Tell me
I'm OK,
really

Rosie Rushton

Piccadilly Press • London

*For Emily Cox, the Bluestones girl, and for all the pupils
of Smithycroft School, Glasgow*

First published in Great Britain in 2000
by Piccadilly Press Ltd.,
5 Castle Road, London NW1 8PR

A catalogue record for this book is available from
the British Library

ISBNs: 1 85340 616 3 (trade paperback)
1 85340 621 X (hardback)

1 3 5 7 9 10 8 6 4 2

Printed and bound by WBC, Bridgend
Jacket design by Louise Millar
Design by Judith Robertson

Set in 12pt Bembo

*Rosie Rushton lives in Northampton. She is the author of a number of
series published by Piccadilly Press, including:*
BEST FRIENDS
THE GIRLS
THE LEEHAMPTON QUARTET
and also the books:
SPEAK FOR YOURSELF
STAYING COOL, SURVIVING SCHOOL,
YOU'RE MY BEST FRIEND, I HATE YOU!
She is co-author of PS HE'S MINE! with Nina Schindler.

CHAPTER ONE

TUESDAY
afternoon

THERE SHE IS, in the chair by the window. She hasn't seen me yet. She's just sitting there, looking vacant. I never thought it was possible for people to sit and look at nothing but believe me, my mother's got it down to a fine art.

In a minute, I'll have to go into the room and start the whole stupid exercise all over again. The "Hi, Mum, how are you today?" bit – I've done it every other day for nearly a month now, and frankly, it's pointless. Dad may say that she loves to see me, but that's a load of nonsense. She doesn't care about me. If she did, she would be at home with me and Dad and not here, being waited on hand and foot in this mental hospital.

I know, I know – you're not supposed to call them mental hospitals. OK, then, a psychiatric hospital. Same difference. A whole load of weird people swanning around in varying degrees of bewilderment or sitting on the floor cross-legged, trying to find themselves.

Not that it looks like a hospital, more like a stately home. There's this huge lawn in front and two stone lions either side of the entrance. It's even got a swimming-pool and health club. She can get her hair done and have massages and everything. No wonder she says she's not ready to come home. She's got it made.

Well, lucky bloody her.

Of course, the doctors say that I mustn't be like this. It's not her fault, that's what they all tell me. It's an illness, just like pneumonia or chickenpox, only this one makes her behave in funny ways and see things differently from the way everyone else sees them. I'll tell you one thing – it's a whole lot more scary than chickenpox.

If it's anyone's fault that she's here, I guess it's mine. She always said I would drive her insane and now I have. I didn't mean it to turn out this way, really I didn't.

"Hi there, Georgie! Come to see your mum, have you?"

No, I've come for a spot of abseiling from the balcony.

"Oh, hi, Miranda. Yes, that's right."

That's Mum's nurse, Miranda Jenks. All the nurses are like her, so flipping cheerful, like it was some holiday camp, all "let's do some macramé" and "keep looking on the positive side". What positive side? That's what I want to know.

"What's that, dear? I didn't quite catch what you said."

Oh, great. She's looking at me all puzzled.

4

"Nothing – just – er, just memorising my French verbs."

I do that all the time now. Talk to myself, as if I'm doing the commentary on a TV documentary with me as the star. I even imagine the cameras rolling and a whole production crew hanging on my every word. I don't do it deliberately; it just happens. And it helps; sometimes, when I feel as if I am going to float away for ever and disappear into nothingness, the sound of my own voice makes me feel real again. I've been talking to myself silently, inside my head, for years; well, no one else bothered listening to me so there didn't seem much point wasting my breath on talking out loud. But then, after Mum started going crazy, everything in my head got in such a muddle that I had to say things out loud to try to make sense of them.

"Off you go then, dear." Miranda gives me a friendly nudge. "We don't want to keep Mum waiting, do we?"

Suddenly I want to scream at the stupid nurse, make her see that the woman sitting in that chair staring blankly at nothing isn't my mum. She may look like her, she may be wearing her clothes, but it's not her.

It's just a shell.

A shell that looks like she should be Mum. But isn't.

And once I push this door open and walk into that room, I won't be me either.

And that's the scariest part of all.

She's talking today, which is an improvement on when she was first admitted. Well, I say talking – she says a couple of words and I babble on for as long as possible, one eye on the clock, praying for the half-hour to go by quickly.

"School good?"

She glances at me and then looks away again.

"Yeah – great," I lie glibly. No point in telling her that I've got every teacher in the place on my back nagging about falling grades. "I'm going to be Peaseblossom in the school play – *A Midsummer Night's Dream*."

Actually, I'm understudying it and helping shift scenery, but she won't know, will she? And it might make her feel proud.

She nods. "Right."

"And next Tuesday, there's a netball tournament," I say brightly. "So I won't be able to come to see you."

"Right," she says again. Not, "Oh, I'll miss you" or, "Hope your team wins, darling". Just "Right".

I can feel my chest getting tighter. It always does that when I feel angry and I feel very angry right now. Angry with her, angry with me, angry with him.

As if she can read my mind, she raises one eyebrow. "And Dad?" she says.

"He's fine." I spit the words out before my throat closes up and I can't say anything else. As if she really cared.

I get up and walk to the window. It's starting to rain and a couple of manic squirrels are chasing one another round and round the stone fountain. Just watch those. Don't think about Dad. Don't think about the way he has been since it happened. Don't think at all.

"Georgie Girl?"

I turn. She hasn't used my nickname in months. For some reason I suddenly want to cry.

"Yes?"

"You must . . ." She frowns and runs her tongue across her bottom lip as if she's forgotten what she was about to say.

"What?"

I squat down beside her chair.

She takes my hand and leans forward, peering anxiously into my eyes. "You must look after your dad."

I can feel my jaw clenching, even before she has got the words out. Why must I? Why me? That's your job, not mine. Mothers are supposed to cook and clean and wash shirts and do the shopping, and kids are supposed to go out with their mates and snog boys and argue with their parents about curfews. And how come she's so worried about him, all of a sudden? Perhaps if she'd been a bit nicer before, things wouldn't be so awful now. If she'd been more like other mothers . . .

"I've given him a hard time. He needs you, Georgie."

She's looking straight at me, her chin jutting out like it used to when I was little and she got cross with me for wetting my knickers on the leather seats of her car.

"You hear what I say, Georgie?"

Funny how when she wants to make a point she can look almost like her old self.

"Yeah, yeah, OK!" Change the subject. "So, when are you coming home, Mum?"

She looks away at once. Her fingers begin pulling at the lapels of her shirt, her shoulders hunch up round her ears.

"I'm not ready yet," she says. "I can't do it, Georgie. Not yet. I can't!"

With each word her voice becomes more shrill. She starts rubbing her chin, faster and faster as if she is trying to get rid of some invisible smudge of dirt.

"Right," I say. Two can play at that game.

"Right," she repeats, without looking at me. "Right."

I get up. Only five minutes to go. I can safely start making going-home noises now.

"Better get going, then, Mum," I say. "Loads of homework to do – and then I'm going baby-sitting."

Her head jerks round as if yanked by an invisible string. "What?"

"Baby-sitting," I say proudly. "Cool, eh? You know that couple who moved into number fifty-three – the Hollands' old house? Well, they've got this baby boy, Joshua and . . ."

"No, No, No!!!!" The shouts turn to wails, her hands beat up and down on her lap and then, suddenly, without warning, she screams. I mean, an ear-splitting scream. Like a madwoman.

"Mum!"

"Just shut up, Georgie! Just – be quiet!"

She is a madwoman.

In that moment, I know it. My mother isn't temporarily sick, like they say. She isn't just "going through a bad patch". She is mad. Stark, staring, raving mad.

And she hates me. I know she does.

Now she is pacing the room, beating her head with clenched fists as if she's trying to hammer her skull to pieces.

"Mum, stop it! Don't!"

She turns to me, and her mouth is half open and her nose is running with snot and there's blood on her lip.

Suddenly I feel like I'm going to throw up, right there on the carpet. I turn and grab the door handle, but someone has got there before me.

The door bursts open and the nurse, Miranda, rushes in.

"Now, now, Julia, what's all this about?" she says to Mum, in the kind of voice most people reserve for talking to rather dippy four-year-olds. "We can't have this, now can we?"

She takes a firm hold of Mum's arms, sits her down in the chair and murmurs soothingly at her.

Mum rocks herself backwards and forwards, tossing her head from side to side and hugging her arms round her body.

Like before.

Like that Sunday.

I have to get out of this place. I turn and run.

"Georgie, dear – wait!" Miranda's voice wafts down the corridor after me.

I take no notice.

I just keep running.

I hate her, I hate her, I hate her! With every slam of my boots on the wet pavement I can feel the anger boiling up inside me. I imagine her face, all wild-eyed and manic, staring up from every paving stone and I want to stamp on it; I want to scream and tell her that because of her my whole life has been turned upside down and is getting worse every day.

I see her yelling at me because my room's a mess or because I forgot to put the oven on for dinner when she was at yet another of her stupid meetings. Her words echo in my ears in time with the beating of my feet on the pavement – "Georgie, can't you do *anything* right? Georgie, you're not making an effort! Georgie, you're driving me insane!"

I don't stop running even though the further I go, the drier my throat gets and the more my chest hurts. My school bag bumps up and down on my hip as I pound along the street. I want to get as far away from her as I can, as fast as I can. I don't want a mother like that, I don't need a mother like that. I hate her!

And then suddenly I'm on the pavement, sprawled out like a rag-doll, with books spewing out of my school bag and the palms of my hands smarting like crazy.

"Ups-a-daisy, tumble tot!"

And she's there. Mum. Standing over me in her denim pinafore dress with the cream shirt underneath, stretching out a hand. She has bright red nail polish and the gold bangle Dad bought her when my older brother, Simon, was born. And she looks normal.

I struggle to sit up.

"It hurts!" I'm crying and I stretch out my hand.

And she's gone.

I'm sitting on the pavement and the rain is getting heavier. I'm nearly sixteen years old and I've just spoken to a woman who isn't there.

What does that make me?

Mad.

Like her.

When I was little, I wanted to be just like Mum. But not now, not any more.

I've got to get a grip. I'm OK. Really I am. I'm Georgina Eloise Linnington, I live at sixteen Phillimore Gardens and I'm absolutely fine. Truly.

And I didn't mean it when I said I hated my mother. I don't, not really. I love her and I want her here. Now.

But I want her like she used to be.

Then I could be like I used to be and everything would be all right again.

I am about to get up when there is the sound of thudding feet.

"Hey, look who's here! Whatya doin', Georgie – talking to yourself again?"

Two pairs of dirty trainers have stopped by my right knee. I look up. And want to die.

It's Liam Maxwell from school and his mate Jamie, all swagger and sneering faces.

"Always said she was weird," comments Liam, nudging Jamie in the ribs.

I scramble to my feet and grab at the pencils and books scattered over the pavement.

"Yeah," nods Jamie, idly kicking my Geography book out of reach. "Who else would sit on the ground in the pouring rain, talking to thin air?"

I can feel the heat burning my cheeks as I lunge for the book, but Jamie's foot is firmly on it.

"I need that," I say, trying to sound assertive.

"What you need," jeers Liam, slowly blowing bubblegum into my face, "is a brain transplant. Weirdo!"

"I'll tell my brother!"

Even before the words are out I realise what a total idiot I am. I haven't used that threat since I was about ten – and anyway, Simon's hundreds of miles away at university and, as far as I can tell, has totally forgotten that he ever had a sister, never mind wanting to look out for her.

"Oh help me, help me!" sneers Jamie. "I am *so* fwitened!!"

He lisps mockingly and curls his lip at me.

Now I want to cry again and if I let that happen in front of these two, it'll be all round school tomorrow. I abandon the book and start running.

"Mental!" they cry as I turn the corner. "Stark, staring, raving mad!"

"No!" The word is out before I can stop it.

"No, no, no!"

I'm too far away now for them to hear my denial. They probably wouldn't believe it anyway.

Why should they? I don't.

I'm inside the phone box and dialling Simon's number before I realise what I'm doing. I've shoved in a whole one-pound coin, because this time I'm going to make him listen, make him see that he has to come home and sort things out.

Simon's always sorted me out. When we were younger, and I used to get into trouble for wandering off or playing with matches, it was Simon who used to think up the wickedest excuses to get me off the hook. He's six years older than me and he could always twist Mum round his little finger. I guess I might have hated him for that if he hadn't been on my side so often but now, I'm glad he's Mum's favourite. If I can just make him see how bad she is, he'll get on a train and come home and then it won't just be down to me to keep things going.

Just as I think no one is going to answer, there is a click and a girl's voice comes down the line. She sounds half asleep.

"Yeah?"

"Oh, I – er, is Simon Linnington there, please?"

"Who's that?"

The voice is high-pitched and really upper-class snooty.

"His sister, actually."

I'm tempted to add, And who are you when you're at home? but I bite my lip and say nothing. The seconds are ticking away and I just want her to get Simon.

"Sy! Si-mon! Wake up!"

Wake up? It's five o'clock in the afternoon; what's he doing in bed? Oh. No. No, he can't have been. I mean, he wouldn't . . .

"It's your sister – you never said you had a sister."

Oh terrific.

There's a clattering and the sound of muffled yawning.

"Georgie?"

The sound of his voice is enough. I burst into tears.

"Simon – you've got to come home. Mum . . ."

My voice catches on a sob.

"What? What's happened? Is she ill?"

"What do you mean, 'Is she ill'? You know bloody well she's ill – she's in a mental hospital, for God's sake!"

"Sssh!" he hisses at me down the phone. "Don't shout! Hang on!"

His voice goes all muffled and I know he has put his hand over the mouthpiece. I can just hear him muttering to the girl, something about seeing her outside in five minutes. Then she says she'll hang on and there's more whispering that I can't hear. And all the time my money is ticking away in the meter.

"Georgie? Are you still there?"

No, I've just flown to Barbados for a spot of jet-skiing. Of course I'm still here.

"Listen, Mum's really bad, Sy. I mean, you haven't seen her since she went in there. I've just been with her, and she was screaming and shouting and banging her head and . . ."

"She's done that before, Georgie. It's just her way. The

14

hospital will sort it. Don't let it get to you, OK?"

"No, it's not OK!"

My hand is actually shaking as I grip the receiver more tightly. "Simon, I can't handle all this on my own. You've no idea what it's like. It's not just that Mum doesn't seem to want to come home – it's Dad. He's just moping about and I have to organise everything at home and . . ."

I hear this girl chuntering about something in the background, and I can tell, even at this distance, that Simon isn't really listening to me at all. "Look, Georgie, I can't talk now," he says. "Got to dash out."

Oh sure. With her, no doubt.

"But you will come home this weekend? Promise?"

There's a long silence. Too long.

"I can't."

"But you have to!"

"No, I don't. I'm twenty one – I don't *have* to do anything."

I can't believe it. Twenty-one or not, he's still my brother.

"But . . ."

"Look, it's not as if Mum's dying or anything. It's like Dad says – she's just wrung out. Some women go a bit, well, you know – funny – when they get older; it's no big deal."

It is from where I'm standing.

"So you won't come?"

I spit the words out through gritted teeth.

"I can't – I'm going to this party and . . ."

15

"Oh, well, great! What do your own family matter when there's a party to go to? Pardon us for breathing! If you . . ."

"Georgie, grow up, for God's sake! Don't make such a big deal of it all!"

I stop in mid-flow, tears welling up in my eyes. Simon's never been like this with me, never.

"But it is a big deal! Why are you being like this? Simon?"

But all I get in response is the dialling tone.

My brother has hung up.

It's not until some old woman glares at me through the glass door that I realise I am shouting his name and slamming the receiver against the window frame. I hurl it down and it swings wildly back and forth on its coiled cord.

As I push the door open the woman grabs my arm and mutters something about vandalism and public property.

"I know, I shouldn't have done that," I say, switching into my apologetic but tragic mode and imagining the hidden cameras whirring for the benefit of the viewing public. "It's just that I've had the most terrible news about . . . "

I cast my eyes to the ground.

"Well, you see – I'm sorry – I can't . . ."

The woman pats my arm. "It's all right, dear," she says. "I shouldn't have been so quick to judge. God be with you."

I want to tell her that God gave up on me a long time ago, but I don't have the energy. I just smile weakly and start running again.

LATER
that day

There's one good thing about going home to an empty house you don't get the third degree the moment you open the front door. Mum's never been at home much after school — well, not till she went peculiar and chucked in the job — but after Dad got made redundant, he was always hanging around and wanting to know what grades I'd got and whether I'd got a boyfriend yet. And when my mates called round, he would hover and try to join in the conversation, saying really dumb things about boy bands because he thought he sounded trendy. It was dead embarrassing. It came as a great relief when he finally found another job. He moans about it a lot, but at least it keeps him out of the way.

Right now, I'm so angry that I'm glad there's no one around. For once I'm pleased that my parents never got round to buying that stair carpet; the sound of my boots thudding on the wooden boards as I stomp up to my bedroom is somehow very satisfying.

My bedroom is right at the top of the house. In Victorian times it used to be three little rooms, where the servants slept, but when my grandmother died and Mum inherited the house, she and Dad knocked them into one big room. Simon used to have it but when he went off to uni, I bagged it. It seemed like a good idea at the time – to be tucked away under the eaves, in my own private place where I didn't have to listen to the arguing and the crying and everything. Only it didn't quite work out that way.

I kick open the door, hurl my school bag on to the floor and throw myself on to the bed. And there they both are – grinning at me from their silver photo frames on the bedside table. Mum and Simon. Mum's looking straight at me, head thrown back, lips parted, the wind catching her long auburn hair and making her look like the figurehead on one of those old sailing ships. Simon is in profile, which makes him look as if he's staring out of his frame straight at Mum, sharing some joke with her and shutting me out.

For a few seconds, I hardly realise what I'm doing – not until the first photo frame hits the brass handle of the bedroom door, shattering the glass into pieces and skewing the picture half in, half out of the now-dented frame. By the time the second one catches the corner of my dressing-table and smashes, I'm off the bed, snatching the pictures off the floor and ripping them in two.

"I hate you! I hate you! I hate you!"

The torn fragments flutter from my hands like confetti but it's not enough. With a sweep of my arm I clear the top of my dressing-table, sending make-up brushes and bottles and my big chunky candle to the floor. I yank out my underwear drawer and tip the contents on my bed, then my sweater drawer and a whole shelf of paperback books.

Suddenly there's a loud bang. It's the slamming of the front door that brings me up with a jolt. Dad! He'll go ape if he finds out what I've done. I grab a handful of knickers and stuff them back into a drawer.

"Georgie? Georg-ie!!!"

It's not Dad. It's even worse than Dad.

"It's me – Amber!"

I don't believe it. How did she get in? I guess I was in such a state when I got home that I didn't shut the front door properly. And Amber, being Amber, wouldn't think twice about charging in uninvited.

Normally, I wouldn't mind. I mean, Amber's my best friend and everything, but right now I don't want to be with anyone, not even her – not till I've had the chance to sort my head out. And come to think of it, my room as well.

I can hear her thudding up the stairs and I nip on to the landing, kicking a shard of broken glass out of the way so that the door shuts firmly behind me.

And only just in time.

"Georgie!" Amber pants, as she reaches the top of the stairs. "Where the hell were you? You said you'd meet me at Costa Coffee – where did you get to?"

"I – er . . ."

In my panic over Mum I'd completely forgotten about our arrangement to do some window-shopping after school.

Amber peers at me as I grab her arm and practically drag her down the stairs again.

"You look awful," she says. "Have you been crying?"

"Crying?" I try to sound incredulous. "Course not!"

Well, you don't admit to howling your eyes out when you are nearly sixteen. Not that I feel sixteen any more – inside my head, I feel about twelve. Even my body seems to think I'm still a kid. I'm really skinny, and my boobs are too small to show through my sweater. My dad says my hair is my crowning glory; it's auburn like Mum's and really long and thick, but frankly I'd swap it any day for a proper chest. I don't even get a period every month, just off and on, when it feels like coming. I haven't told anyone that, of course, not even Amber. She started while we were still at primary school and wore a bra when she was nine. I did try to mention it to Mum a few months ago, but that was when she had already started going doolally and all she said was, "You don't want to grow up too fast, believe me," which on the Helpful Mother stakes rated about minus five.

"So what happened?" Amber peers at me as we clatter down the stairs. "How come it took so long?"

I struggle to remember what excuse I made for skipping netball practice this time. The dentist, that was it.

"Fillings," I mumble, clutching my jaw in what I hope is a suitably pained manner. "He found three. Absolute agony. Sorry."

"Poor you," sighs Amber with a slight shudder. "Let's see."

"They're white ones, you won't see a thing!" I shove her across the hall and into the kitchen. "Anyway, what are you doing here?"

Her face breaks into this broad grin and she gives herself a hug. "It's happened!" she exclaims. "He's done it!"

"Who's done what?" I yank open the fridge and give my jaw another tentative rub, just for good measure.

"Nick, stupid!" she replies. "I bumped into him on the way over here and guess what? He's asked me out. Tonight."

"Oh. Right."

"Right? Right? The fittest boy in the whole of Year Eleven asks me out on a date and all you can say is 'right'?"

Oh, God, I'm sounding like my mother. They say when you live with people you end up like them.

"Sorry – that's great," I say, trying to sound excited. "Really. Ace."

I give her what I hope is an enthusiastic grin, and shove a can of lemonade into her hands.

"Dead right it is," affirms Amber, ripping back the ring pull. "I am just so in love, I can't breathe. Know what I mean?"

Oh sure. Am I likely to know? I've never had a boy-friend, never mind fallen in love. I had the chance, once.

With Philip Waterman. But I blew it. I do that a lot. Blow things.

"Mmm," I murmur non-committally.

"So, will you do my hair?" Amber pleads, running her fingers impatiently through her thick, unruly curls. "I look like a poodle that got caught in a thunderstorm."

I can't help giggling. Her description is so apt.

"Oh, good, you *can* laugh!" teases Amber. "I was beginning to think something really mega tragic had happened."

Just for a moment, I want to tell her everything. I want to stop pretending and blurt it all – about Mum, the hospital, about what had happened that Sunday and how, because of that, I'm supposed to look after Dad and make things all right for him. It is as much as I can do not to scream at her, shake her, make her see how lucky she is to have nothing more important to worry about than a stupid hairstyle and some dumb boy.

Of course, I don't say a word. I do my usual trick of biting the inside of my cheek really hard and putting my tongue right back on the roof of my mouth and imagining all the words I want to say being swallowed, one after the other down my throat and into oblivion. All right, it sounds crazy, but it works, OK? It's better than saying things you will regret later. I know what I'm talking about. Believe me.

Do you think that makes me mad?

"Georgie!" Amber is shaking my arm. "This is no time to go off in one of your trances. Nick's calling for me at seven o'clock and I haven't even done my underarms yet. So can we get a move on?"

I'm so eager to quell her idea that I spend half my life on another planet that I've nodded my agreement before I realise it.

"Ace!" she says. "Come on, let's go up to your room."

She's pounding back up the stairs, babbling something about Nick's thigh muscles and how his hair curls round his ears.

And there's nothing I can do about it.

"We'll do it in the bathroom," I cry, as we reach the landing. "You go in and I'll collect the mousse and stuff."

"No, silly," Amber retorts. "We need a socket to plug in the tongs."

That's that then. She's almost at my bedroom door and I had better start thinking really fast.

Amber thinks my bedroom is great which is odd really, because it is not nearly as wacky as her own. Her mum is a sculptress and she makes the wildest things – not just boring plaster heads and stuff, but huge ceramic hands with giant-sized fingers for you to stick on the wall and hang your clothes from, and doorstops in the shape of question marks and mirrors decorated with china letters and messages like "Oh Boy, Am I Gorgeous!" on them. Amber says all that stuff's OK, but it doesn't change the fact that not only is her mum's room right next door, which puts paid to late-night phone calls and loud music, but her room overlooks a cemetery and there's not much excitement in looking at a row of headstones week after week.

I've got three windows in my room, one from each of the old servants' rooms, and each one has a window seat. One looks over our back garden, one over the street in front of the house and the third one directly into The Wilderness. That's what we call the house next door because it has been empty for years and the garden is a total mess, in a rather pretty, rambling sort of way.

Usually the first thing Amber does when I open my bedroom door is rush over to the window to peer out and launch into her Great Plan. She has had this plan for weeks now, ever since Nick Trevelyan came to our school and Amber decided that he was without doubt going to be the love of her life.

"It's destiny," she told me on the second day of term, with all the self-assurance of someone with a huge chest and cheekbones to die for. "I can feel it here."

She had clamped her fist to her heart and sighed. "And that," gesturing towards The Wilderness, "is where it is all going to happen."

"You have to be joking!" I had cried. "For one thing, he hasn't asked you out and for another, I can hardly see him wanting to spend time hacking his way through overgrown shrubbery."

"You," Amber had retorted, "have no soul. It won't be like that. He will ask me out – and then one day, I'll bring him round to your house, and you'll be in floods of tears . . ."

"I'll *what*?"

I may cry a lot these days, but I don't do it to order and certainly not in front of a boy.

"Listen!" she had replied impatiently. "You'll be crying because you've dropped your favourite ring, or bracelet or something out of the window into The Wilderness . . ."

"Oh, very probable!" I had exclaimed but she ignored me as usual.

". . . and I'll say, 'Nick and I will find it' and then we'll go over the fence and start crawling about in the bushes and I'll brush my cheek against his and then . . ."

At that point I had switched off. Not only was the idea totally ludicrous, but Amber is inclined to go into the most intimate details when it comes to her future plans for the male population of Wheatley Hill High, and since the closest I've ever got to passion is a slurpy kiss from Philip Waterman (a kiss somewhat marred by his garlic breath), listening to Amber does nothing for my self-esteem.

"Georgie! What on earth . . . ?"

She's opened the door and stopped dead, her mouth wide open in amazement. No chance of any window seat fantasising now.

It's not the mess on the bed that's got her attention; she knows how untidy I can be. Her eyes are fixed firmly on the smashed photo frames. "Georgie, what's been going on?" She's down on her knees, picking through the debris. "What's happened to these?"

Already I've switched into TV commentator mode, and the videotape is running in my head.

"Georgie?" She holds out a piece of photograph, with Mum's face sliced in half.

I smile, even though there is a lump in my throat the size of a walnut. I look at the picture, but all I can see is Mum's face, contorted and twisted, yelling at me in the hospital bedroom. And Amber keeps staring at me.

"Oh, that!" I say in a matter-of-fact sort of way. "There's this competition next week at Mum's office – Guess The Employee. Everyone has to take in a picture of just a part of their face and then the staff have to guess who it is."

I'm getting incredibly good at spontaneous lying. I amaze myself sometimes.

Amber frowns.

"And," I continue hastily, "Mum's so busy with work and stuff that she asked me to get it organised."

You can never be too sure that someone believes you until you have embellished the story a little.

Amber doesn't look too convinced. "But this is all smashed. It's the picture you had by your bed – the one when your mum won that award."

I shrug my shoulders, desperately trying to ignore the sound of Mum's shouting that is pounding louder and louder in my ears.

"That was ages ago," I say as lightly as I can, "she's changed heaps since then."

And how.

Amber's eyes scan the rest of the room and end up back on the shards of broken glass by the dressing-table.

I can see she hasn't finished her interrogation and decide to get in first.

"See, I was having this mega huge clear-out of my stuff," I say, waving an arm expansively round the room. "And I was yanking out my bedside drawer when my elbow caught the photo and it smashed."

Her eyes don't leave my face. To avoid her gaze, I bend down, pick up some of the bigger shards of glass and dump them in my waste bin.

"So, I thought, what the hell – I'll use that photo and get another one of Mum to replace it."

"But what about that . . . ?"

She points to the fragments of Simon's picture.

"Once I got going, I thought I'd have a revamp," I smile. "Feng Shui and all that – Simon's picture is way out of date."

Amber's eyes narrow and I know she doesn't believe me. "But . . ."

"Hey – is that the time?" I gesture towards the clock on my wall. "Do you want your hair done or not?"

"Oh my God!" Amber cries, dashing over to the dressing-table. "I'll never be ready. Quick. Do something!"

Thank heavens for Amber's obsession with her love life.

"Tongs or hot brush?" I ask with relief.

"I told you, tongs," replies Amber. "I want to look sort of soft and vulnerable and yet alluring and mysterious."

"Right!" I plug in the tongs.

"Do you think little curls over my forehead and tendrils caressing my ears?" she asks.

She's prone to talking like a romantic novel when she is in love. Which is pretty much all the time.

"Sure," I nod, grabbing the styling brush. "Mum's got this wicked Freeze and Shine spray . . ."

How dumb can you get? I'd just got her to shut up about my mother and here I go, mentioning her all over again.

"I haven't seen your mum for ages," she says, peering in the mirror and molesting a small zit.

"She's away," I reply shortly, picking up a strand of her hair. "On business."

"Where?"

"Hong Kong."

I don't know why I said that, really I don't. I mean, I could just as easily have said Manchester or Paris, but the words came out of my mouth before I knew anything about it. I guess it's OK; Mum was Businesswoman of the Year for East Anglia four years ago, and people still expect her to be hurtling around the globe closing deals.

Amber is clearly impressed.

"Wow!" she exclaims. "I'd die to go there! So exotic! When's she coming home?"

"Not sure – these deals take their time."

I'm getting into the swing of it now.

"Still, she'll be home for your birthday, won't she?" Amber asks eagerly. "I can't wait to find out what she's got planned, can you?"

I wish she hadn't said that. Now I can feel the floaty feeling coming on, and I just want to get the hell out of this bedroom and curl up somewhere and forget birthdays and mad mothers and how things ought to be. Forget that in just a week's time I'll be sixteen and that everyone in my year is expecting an invitation to the amazing celebration that I've convinced them will be happening.

"I can bring Nick, can't I?" Amber goes on. "To whatever it is."

Or isn't.

"Sure."

This is getting out of hand. I ought to come clean. But I can't.

I wind a strand of Amber's hair round the tongs and yank it.

"Ouch!" Amber yells. "That hurt!"

"Sorry."

"Just get on with it."

She picks up my new copy of *Heaven Sent* and begins flicking through the pages. Hopefully that article on Ten Ways To Seduce Your Lover will shut her up for bit. I won't be able to keep thinking up excuses for much longer. If my mother doesn't get off her backside and get better and start acting normal, someone will find out the truth. But I can't let that happen. She is my mum, after all, no matter what she's like now.

As I pile Amber's unruly hair on to the top of her head with a big clip, I think about the time when Mum used to sit me on a pile of cushions and braid my hair, and sing songs to me. That was in the days when everything was

OK, before the rows started and the long silences; before Mum spent all her time rushing around doing business and getting stressed.

Back then, you would never have guessed that Mum was going to go crazy or that Dad would turn out to be so – well, feeble.

He is, though. Totally feeble. I mean, I love him to bits, and I feel really sorry for him, in an annoyed kind of way – but when Mum started going funny, he pretended it wasn't happening – even though a moron could see something was wrong.

"It'll all be fine," he used to say. "It's just her age, love. Don't worry your head about it."

And then, when it was quite clear that it wasn't fine at all, he expected me to take over where Mum left off. And I can't do it and . . .

"GEORGIE! You're scorching my hair!"

Amber has snatched the tongs from my hand and slammed them down on the dressing-table.

"What's with you?" she demands, jutting out her pointed chin and glaring at me. "You haven't heard a word I've been saying and you've curled the same piece of hair three times!"

"Sorry – I was miles away."

"Yes, well I could see that!" she retorts. "You had that look on your face."

"What look?"

"Your dippy, totally out of it, away with the fairies

look," she replied. "The one you wear half the time these days. What's wrong with you?"

"Nothing," I lie. "So go on, tell me about Nick!"

It's not that I am the slightest bit interested in the finer points of her love life, but listening to her stops me thinking too closely about what might be wrong with me.

"He is so gorgeous," she sighs, handing me the tongs and gesturing to me to get on with it. "He's not like any boy I've ever known."

"You always say that," I mutter, picking up a hairbrush and squirting it with hairspray. "You said Matt was your soul mate and Andrew could read your mind and . . ."

"Yes, well, this really is different," she insists. "Nick is so much more mature – and he understands my complex psyche."

"Your what?"

"He says I am a multi-faceted personality. That's what attracted him to me."

"You mean," I tease her, "that he has discovered that you want one thing one day and something totally different the next!"

Amber raises an eyebrow and doesn't laugh like she's meant to. "Well," she says, "at least I'm not boring!"

"Meaning I am?" I can hear the edginess in my own voice.

"No," she murmurs, in a not totally convincing manner. "But you are a bit . . ."

"What?"

"Well . . . don't get me wrong, Georgie, but lately –
well, you've changed. You've been acting a bit weird."

I bite my lip and try to look unconcerned.

"It's mixing with you that does it," I reply glibly. I'd read
this book that says that when people get to you, all you
have to do is make a joke of things and they'll change the
subject. I don't think it's going to work on Amber.

"Oh, ha ha!" she replies. "No, honestly, I'm kind of
worried about you."

"Why?" I switch off the tongs and brush her hair into
shape.

"It's like you don't care any more. You daydream your
way through lessons, people talk to you and you look
straight through them as if they are not there, and you
mutter a lot . . . Will that do for starters?"

My heart starts racing and I can feel my jaw clenching.
She's going off me, just like everyone else has, and she's the
one real mate I've got left. If she ditches me because I'm
going loopy, what will I do?

Anyway, it's not fair. She doesn't know the half of it.
Who does she think she is, sitting there making snide
remarks? Her with her normal mother and dishy boyfriend
and straight A grades.

"Oh, well terrific!" I hurl the hairbrush on to the
dressing-table and turn away. "Well, your hair's done so
you'd better go, hadn't you? After all, you don't want to
spend time with a weirdo, do you?"

I can feel my cheeks burning and I've got this

overwhelming desire to trash the room all over again.

"Georgie!" Amber jumps up, frowning. "I didn't mean it like that . . ."

"So how did you mean it, then?"

"I'm just worried about you." She touches my arm and I jerk it away. "You do crazy things and I worry about you. You are my best friend, after all."

So she still likes me. So maybe it's OK. Maybe I'm over-reacting. I smile, imagining the TV cameras trained on my face. Brave, gutsy Georgie Linnington, soldiering on in the face of extreme adversity.

The imaginary cameras pan in closer. I tilt my chin in a dignified manner. "I'm OK – it's just . . ." I drop my eyes and leave a dramatic pause.

"Just what?" Now Amber's looking genuincly concerned.

"I've got a few health problems right now – I've got to have tests and stuff, and . . ."

I didn't mean to say that, honestly I didn't. It just happened. The words just came – but now I can see how anxious Amber looks, I know I won't stop.

"Tests? What tests?" she gasps.

"Oh – nothing much – just a few things not quite right. I guess that's why I've been a bit distracted lately."

I run my tongue along my bottom lip and hope that I look sad but rather heroic.

Amber puts an arm round my shoulders and gives me a little squeeze.

"Georgie, I'm *really* sorry! I wouldn't have said what I

did if I had known – what's wrong with you?"

I've got a mother who's gone crazy, a father who's turning into a world class drip and I'm going slowly mad. Apart from that, everything's cool.

"I don't really want to talk about it, not right now . . ."

"But I'm your friend!" Amber looks hurt.

"I will tell you," I assure her. "Just give me time to get used to it all. Please."

And to think up a good story.

"Besides," I add hurriedly, "you'd better get going. Don't want to be late for the hot date!"

I open the door and push her through.

"But . . . ?"

"What are you going to wear?" I gabble. "Your leather miniskirt or the blue dress? I reckon the skirt – you look dead sexy in that!"

"I do?" Amber sounds pleased and I know I've hit the spot. "I mean, it doesn't make my bum look too big?"

"No, it's terrific, honestly! Especially with the black boots and . . ."

The walls judder as the front door slams violently.

"Georgie, there you are!"

As we clatter down the final flight of stairs, there's Dad, standing in the hall, looking damp and dishevelled.

"Oh – hi there, Amber! How's it going, dude? Gimme five!"

I do wish my father would stop acting like an ageing adolescent.

"Hi, Mr Linnington," grins Amber. "How are you?"

"Wet," says my father, which was about as accurate a description of himself as you can get. "It's tipping it down out there. You must have got soaked, Georgie, coming back from the . . ."

"I'm fine!" I say hastily. "Out of the way, Dad. Amber's in a rush – she's got a date."

"Have you now?" Dad raises a quizzical eyebrow and gives her his matey-matey grin. "And who's the lucky guy?"

"No one you know," I interject hastily, pushing him out of the way and opening the front door. "See you, Amber."

But Amber has stopped to fiddle with the zip on her jacket.

Dad shrugs his arms out of his raincoat. "So," he says, turning to me, "how was Mum?"

Out of the corner of my eye I can see Amber looking at me in surprise. I fix a bright smile on my lips.

"Fine," I say as calmly as I can. "Not that we talked for long – bad line."

To my relief, Amber wins the battle of the zip and heads for the door.

"Bad line?" Dad's forehead puckered in a frown. "Oh, Georgie, you didn't just phone her, did you? You promised faithfully that you would go and . . ."

"Bye, Amber! Have a brill evening! See you tomorrow!"

She's giving me a really strange look, but I push her down the three tiled steps on to the path and slam the door.

I turn to confront Dad, but he gets in first.

"Georgie, how could you? You know how much Mum likes to see you and . . ."

"Oh sure!" I push past him into the kitchen. "She likes to see me so bloody much that she doesn't talk to me, doesn't ask me things – and then she starts yelling and screaming just because I tell her I'm going baby-sitting."

He frowns.

"You told her *what*?"

"Told her I was sitting for a baby, looking after a kid," I snap back. "Joshua – down the road."

"You actually told your mother that?" He looks as astonished as if I had mentioned that I was planning to take a short flight to Mars. "Why would you do that?"

"Because it was something to talk about!" I retort. "Why not?"

He stares at me for a long moment and then shakes his head slowly. "No reason."

He slumps down at the kitchen table and sighs deeply. If I give him half a chance, he'll launch into a tale of woe about how he hates this new job and how things aren't like they used to be, so I ignore him.

"I'm in a hurry, so we need supper – like now!" I tell him.

"Oh – right." He doesn't move. Clearly if we are going to eat, it is down to me. Again. I'm getting good at cooking; heaven knows I've had enough practise.

"So anyway," he says, "you did go? To the hospital?"

"Yes!" I spat the word out, yanking open the fridge and hurling some sausages and bacon on to the table. "Much

36

good it did me. Dad, it was awful. She went ballistic –
banging her fists, shaking her . . ."

He waves a hand to shut me up.

"So what was all that rubbish about a bad line?"

"What do you think it was all about?" I storm,
wrenching the wrapper off the sausages. "Amber was
standing right beside me! How could you be so stupid as
to go on and on about visiting Mum in front of her? It
could have kept for five minutes!"

"But I wanted to know how . . ."

"But I don't want my mates to know that my mother is
locked up in a loony bin! Do you think I'm proud of the
fact that she's mental? Because if you do, you're as daft as
she is!" I turn away and grab the frying-pan in a desperate
attempt not to cry.

"Georgie! Don't say that! She is not locked up and she's
not mental!"

"Oh get real, Dad! OK, so she's in a psychiatric hospital
being treated for depression and post-traumatic something
or other. It's all the same thing – and it's hardly something
you boast about to the entire universe, is it?"

Dad shakes his head in a bewildered fashion. "But you
can't keep it a secret for ever," he says, "and besides,
Amber's your best friend!"

"So? What's that got to do with anything? And why
can't we keep it a secret? It's no one else's business! I bet
you haven't told anyone at the office about your crazy
wife, have you?"

Dad sighs and puts his head in his hands. It occurs to me that he is badly in need of a decent haircut.

"I have, actually. I have to talk about it to somebody, Georgie," he mutters. "I can't keep it all bottled up inside."

I don't believe this. I mean, it's not as if Dad works here in Kettleborough; he commutes to Leehampton each day and none of his colleagues ever come to our house. No one need ever know.

"What? Are you saying you've actually told them?"

I slosh some oil into the pan and turn up the gas. Dad nods. "Just a couple," he agrees, rubbing his eyes wearily. "I can't live a lie, Georgie. I've been to hell and back these last few weeks – you can't imagine what it's been like for me."

I want to yell at him and say that it hasn't exactly been a picnic for me either, but instead I stab the sausages as viciously as I can and hurl them into the pan.

"Onions or mushrooms?" I growl, turning to face Dad.

He doesn't reply.

"I said, onions or . . ."

Dad's crying. I mean, really crying. His shoulders are heaving and these great, gulping sobs burst out, and he puts his head on the table.

I don't know what to do. I've never seen Dad cry before: not even when Mum was in one of her awful rages. It's my fault; I shouldn't have gone on at him like that. I should have kept my mouth shut.

I wait for a moment but he doesn't stop. I turn down the gas and go over to him and sort of hover.

"Dad?" I touch him tentatively on the shoulder and he looks up.

"I'm sorry," he says, taking my hand. "It's just that without your mum here, nothing seems right."

He sniffs and wipes his nose with the back of his hand. I have a tremendous urge to tell him to use his handkerchief.

"Oh, Georgie, if I didn't have you, I don't know what I'd do."

He pulls me on to his lap and gives me a squeeze and somehow I wish he wouldn't.

"And we're doing OK, aren't we?" he says. "You and me – we'll be all right?"

"Sure."

I have to say that. One parent falling apart is enough for anyone to cope with.

He nods and sniffs. "Was Mum – well, did she seem better today?"

I dig my fingernails into the palms of my hands until it hurts. Hasn't he listened to a single word I've been saying?

"I told you, Dad," I say, pulling away from him and grabbing a knife from the dresser drawer. "She had this screaming fit, banging her head and everything."

Just thinking about it makes me feel sick.

"I expect she was overtired," he says. "She gets emotional when she's weary."

Can you believe that?

"Oh yeah," I mutter sarcastically, chopping mushrooms for all I'm worth. "That'll be it for sure."

"But Georgie," he adds, "don't talk about baby-sitting again, will you? I mean, not while she's like this."

Now what's he on about?

"Why not?"

He clears his throat and drums his fingers up and down on the tablecloth.

"Dad?"

"Well, you know . . ."

"No, I don't know. What are you talking about?"

I throw the mushrooms and bacon into the pan, and turn to face him.

He chews his lip and picks at the edge of the tablecloth.

"Well, Mum's been keen to have another baby, you see, and . . ."

I am so gobsmacked that I drop the knife on to the floor. "She what?"

Mum was hardly ever around for the kids she did have; why would she want more? And besides, she's too old. She's forty-five, for heaven's sake.

Dad sighs. "She misses Simon, you know, now he's at university and . . ."

"She's got me!"

Clearly I'm not enough. I know that Mum and me haven't exactly been getting on this last year or two but I'm not that bad, and I'm certainly better company than some yelling baby.

Dad picks at the tablecloth and sighs again. "Oh yes, I know, love, but you see, she wants another child before it's too late," he says. "Someone to keep her feeling your needed and . . ."

"That's bullshit!" The word is out before I can stop it and Dad jumps to his feet.

"Georgina!" he shouts. "You will not use language like that in this house!"

"OK, it's rubbish, nonsense, call it what you like!" I scream. "If she wants to feel needed, let her come home right now, because she's needed here. But I guess we don't count; she wants someone new to fuss over. She must be out of practice – she's hardly done much fussing over us, has she?"

Dad slumps back into his chair. "That's been my fault, Georgie," he says with that hangdog expression I know so well. "I haven't been the sort of husband she wanted. With me being so useless . . ."

He sighs at this point and bites his lip. ". . . she's had to put all her energies into her career and now she's all burned out. If I had been able to earn more . . ."

Here we go again. I can't stand it.

"Yeah, yeah, OK," I mutter.

But he hasn't finished. "I guess she thought the one thing I could do for her was give her another child," he sighs. "But it hasn't happened, and hearing you talking about babies must have been very hard for her."

Oh great. So now it's all my fault.

"Well, I wasn't to know, was I?" I shout, tipping the bacon, sausages and mushrooms on to plates. "Who in their right mind would want a kid at her age? Not, of course, that she's in her right mind."

"Don't say that, Georgie!"

Oh cripes, he's off again.

"I miss her," he sobs. "I just can't function without her."

"It'll be OK," I say, not because I really believe it but because it might make him feel better. I don't like him crying like this; it's as if all of a sudden I'm the grown-up and he's the kid. And I don't want to be grown up - not if this is as good as it gets.

"You're so like your mum, you know," he mumbles, wiping his nose with the back of his hand.

This I do not need to hear. I dump his supper in front of him and flop down at the opposite end of the table.

"I can't believe you'll be sixteen next week," he sighs.

I can't let this opportunity slip by.

"About my birthday, Dad," I begin, with the widest smile I can manage under the circumstances. "Mum said I could have a party and I was wondering . . ."

"A party?" he gasps. "Well, of course, if things had been different, she would have arranged something nice but . . ."

"Yes, but you see, you won't have to do anything," I add hastily. "You could go out and I can have . . ."

"Georgie, how can you even think of having a party with Mum in hospital?" he demands. "How can you be so self-centred?"

"I just thought . . ."

"We can't celebrate while she's – well, while she's away."

I bite my tongue and do the word-swallowing trick again. "Right," I say, even though I'd like to say a whole lot more.

Dad sighs again. "I'll take you out for a pizza, OK? With Amber? That would be fun, wouldn't it?"

Oh sure. Hardly in the same league as Caitlin's beach barbecue with fireworks or Emily's black tie do. I don't waste my breath on a reply.

"Sixteen, eh? A couple more years and you'll be off to university — and then where will I be?"

I pour some lemonade but my hand is shaking and I manage to slop half of it on to the table.

"You'll have Mum," I say. "And probably a screaming toddler. That should do for starters."

I stab a sausage.

"Who knows?" he says. "Things could get a whole lot worse before they get better. Sometimes I think my life has changed for ever. I just can't bear it."

That does it. I don't want to hear any more. I don't want to be here, listening to him wallowing in self-pity. So I go. Oh, I still sit there, stuffing sausages, bacon and mushrooms into my mouth and slurping lemonade, but in my head I just float away. I do that when things get tough. When I was little, I used to pretend I had shrunk to the size of one of my Duplo people and I would gaze round the room and imagine that I was creeping into an empty milk bottle and peering out at the world. Of course I don't do that any more.

But I do switch off. It's clouds at the moment. Different coloured clouds. This time it's a fluffy, lilac-coloured one that just lifts me out of the kitchen and wafts me up through the ceiling and away. I imagine the whole cloud enveloping me and shutting me off from the world – from the kitchen, and Dad's chuntering, and from the memory of Mum, sitting and rocking backwards and forwards and never once looking me in the eye.

But even the cloud won't blot out the thought that I'm not enough. That Mum wanted another baby, just because Simon's gone away. And that the thought of being left with only me at home was enough to drive her crazy.

Just like she said it would.

I have to stop thinking about it, so even though it is far too early, I get up and leave to go baby-sitting.

And I take my cloud with me. It's easier that way.

I'm halfway across the front garden of The Wilderness, still wrapped in my lilac-coloured fog and aiming for the short cut through the broken section of fence by the back gate, when I walk slap-bang into a faceful of leaves.

"Oh, how wonderful!"

I'm startled out of my daydreaming by what appears to be a talking tree.

"You know, there I was asking God for a bit of help, and hey presto! Here you are! He really is most awfully prompt at times!"

A round, rather red face peers out from behind what I

can now see is a huge green plant growing up a pole. The face beams at me.

"Do be a dear and hang on to this for me, just for a sec!" A large terracotta pot is thrust into my hands with such force that I have no choice but to take it. When you come down from a cloud, it takes a few minutes to get yourself together again.

"Splendid! Now don't move!"

"That's hardly likely," I mutter, staggering slightly under the weight of the plant.

The owner of the red face gives a loud throaty chuckle, slams the door of an exceedingly battered-looking VW Beetle, and bounds up the steps to the front door. She is a very large woman with a great mass of silver hair piled on top of her head and held in place with what looks like a faded peacock feather. She is wearing emerald green velvet trousers and a luminous pink silk overshirt and has a white feather boa slung round her neck. She looks like an outsized ice-cream conc.

"There's no one in," I volunteer as she reaches the front door. "The house has been empty for ages."

"Not any more," she calls, waving a key on the end of a piece of string. "It's mine now!"

And with that, she rams the key into the lock and pushes open the front door.

"Now," she cries enthusiastically, hurtling back down the steps. "Between us we can get this thing into the hallway. I'll go backwards, you steer – OK?"

Somehow we manhandle the plant into the house, kicking piles of junk mail and freebie newspapers out of our way, and dump it in a corner.

"Masterly!" the woman cries, wiping her hands on her trousers. "Flavia, by the way."

"The plant?"

"No, dear, me. Flavia Mott. The plant's an epipremnum." She strokes one of its leaves affectionately.

"Come to think of it, Flavia does sound a bit like a herbaceous plant, doesn't it? Father named me. I had yellow hair when I was born, apparently."

It strikes me that I am destined to be surrounded by raving lunatics for the rest of my life.

Flavia grins. "Latin," she says. "*Flavus* – yellow. Father was very into the Classics."

Bully for Father. I edge my way towards the door.

"And you are?" Flavia is eyeing me expectantly.

"Georgina Linnington," I say, avoiding her gaze. "I live next door."

"Oh splendid!" She claps her hands ecstatically. "My new neighbour! Mother, father, sisters, brothers?"

The nosy type. No way am I getting into that game.

"Mmm," I murmur vaguely. "Sorry, I can't stop – I'm baby-sitting."

"Dear me, and I've kept you!" she cries. "No notion of time – that's always been my problem."

She steps aside as I scuttle through the door. "Thanks so much for your help," she calls after me. "I'm moving in properly tomorrow – do pop in. You can meet Harry."

For just a second, I wonder whether Harry is some really fit guy of about eighteen who will fall passionately in love with me at first sight and wipe the smug smiles off the faces of all my mates who are on to their fifth boyfriend of the year. But then I realise that this Mott woman must be seventy if she's a day and hardly likely to have a teenage son. Harry is probably her husband; I can see him now in my mind's eye: bald head, felt slippers and one of those awful knitted cardigans.

"Well, actually, I can't because . . ."

She doesn't appear to be listening. "Oh, and do feel free to trespass across my front garden any time!"

I turn round and fix an apologetic expression on to my face. "I'm really sorry," I begin. "It's just that this house has been empty for ages and . . ."

"Dear me, I'm not cross!" she beams. "I was just teasing – heaven knows, it's such a mess you can't do any harm. Mind you, I've got plans for it – great plans – but I'm starting on the back garden first."

"That won't please Amber!" I hear myself say.

"Amber, dear?"

"Oh, nothing," I mumble. "Must dash."

She steps back into the hallway and raises a hand. "Till tomorrow, then!"

And with that she shuts the door.

Of course, I shan't go back tomorrow, or any other day for that matter. The last thing I want is for her to get all matey and start inviting herself round for coffee and asking to meet my mum. I'll just make sure I walk on the other side of the road in future.

I just want to be left alone.

Besides, she is clearly quite dotty.

Baby-sitting used to be fun. I mean, babies are a bit boring but I like little kids. I can get inside their heads. Mrs Holland, the woman I used to sit for, said I had a real gift and ought to train to be a nanny. But I shan't do that – I don't want to live in other people's houses and have to do what they say all the time. I've had enough of that at home.

Sitting for the Hollands used to be cool because they had three kids aged two, three and five, and one of them was always awake and wanting a story or a cuddle so you never got bored. Mrs Holland recommended me to the Carters when they moved in. They've only got Joshua, who's ten months old and has been sleeping ever since I got here, which is no fun at all.

Mrs Carter's not exactly a bundle of laughs either. She's given me this long list of dos and don'ts – don't give Josh any juice, do make sure he's got his blue rabbit, don't let him lie in a draught, do sing "Ring-a-Roses" if he wakes up, don't have the TV on too loud, do check him every fifteen minutes . . .

I'm really bored. If I had remembered to bring my homework with me, I could have kept busy thinking about the effects of the Industrial Revolution, but when you're wrapped in a cloud you tend to overlook mundane things like essays and coursework until it's too late.

I switch on the television. ITV has got football and if there is one thing I cannot stand, it's football; BBC 2 and Channel 4 are both gardening programmes and BBC 1 has got some boring politician jabbering on about a mini budget. I'm about to go upstairs and have another attempt at waking Joshua, when I press a button and zap myself to UK Gold.

Great. It's "Casualty". It's already started but it looks as if it might be good. Quite a rough night in Accident & Emergency, by the look of it. That dishy doctor with the designer stubble is chatting up the new receptionist when this guy comes crashing through the doors of the A & E department, dragging this woman who is screaming and pulling off her clothes and trying to bite his arm.

"She just flipped and went crazy!" he shouts as the camera pans in on a close-up of this blathering woman. "She hit me!"

And suddenly I'm not at fifty-three Phillimore Gardens any more and I'm not fifteen.

I'm on the beach with sand in my eyes and the sound of screaming in my ears. I'm ten and I'm scared.

Dead scared.

We always went to Norfolk for our holidays when Simon and I were younger. My parents took a cottage in Burnham Market and we used to spend days messing about in boats at Brancaster Staithe or lolling on Holkham Beach, while Dad indulged in his hobbies – painting rather badly and taking photographs of seabirds – and Mum read books and Simon and I played complicated games or built massive fortresses in the sand. We did the same things every year, and it was great. Everyone knew us, and we knew everyone, and it felt so safe.

But then one year, Simon said he didn't want to go any more. Said it was boring and a little kid's holiday place and that he was fourteen and deserved something more exciting. I remember that Mum cried a lot and said the family was breaking up, and Dad said that was silly and Simon was right – boys of his age needed to be with their mates. In the end, Simon went off on this adventure holiday to the Lake District, abseiling and canoeing and stuff, and Dad, Mum and me went to Norfolk. And it was all wrong from the beginning.

For one thing, Mum just worked all the time. She took her laptop and shut herself in the back room of the cottage and left Dad and me to go to the beach on our own. Dad tried to pretend it was fun, but you could see he was miserable. We'd end up going home early and Mum would grumble and say that she hadn't expected us back yet and why couldn't we find something else to do?

Every morning she would phone Simon in Windermere and every evening he phoned her. If he was even ten minutes late calling, she'd start pacing up and down the room, looking at her watch and getting more and more stressed out. She would turn on Dad and say that she just knew something had happened to him, and why hadn't he stopped him going? Then Sy would phone, and Mum would be all smiles till the next time. But she never stopped working.

One time Dad just walked into the room and yanked the plug out of the socket so that the screen on her laptop went dead.

"This is meant to be a holiday," he said. "I've got a great idea – let's . . ."

But I never found out what the idea was because Mum jumped up out of her chair, grabbed the coffee mug that was on the table and hurled it at him. Then she began beating Dad's chest with her fists and calling him a fool and a useless lump and a load of other horrible things, and I shouted and burst into tears and screamed at her to leave him alone.

"Get upstairs!" she yelled at me and I can see her now, tears coursing down her cheeks and her mouth twisted into a weird shape. I didn't want to leave Dad, but Mum kept screaming so I went anyway.

No one said anything about it after that, and for the next few days we all went out together. We had picnics and went to stately homes and took a boat out to see the seals off Blakeney Point, and Dad laughed and told silly jokes and Mum smiled vacantly – but all the time there was this tense atmosphere, as if we were polite strangers not knowing quite how to treat one another.

It was the day before we were due to go home that I got lost. I'd been playing hide-and-seek with a couple of kids I'd bumped into on the beach, and I had wandered off into the pine woods behind the sand dunes to find a good hiding-place. Being me, I started pretending; first I was an explorer hacking my way through uncharted territory in order to find a lost city, then I was a world famous naturalist, risking life and limb to seek out a rare species of tiger. By the time I had become the heiress to a fortune, kidnapped by ruthless bounty hunters, I was totally and completely lost.

I wasn't stupid. I faced the sea and started walking. The wind had got up and sand was blowing in my face, stinging my cheeks and making my eyes water. I kept squinting in an attempt to see Mum and Dad, but Holkham Beach is vast and the tide was out and every patch of sand looked the same.

"Found you, found you!" Tamsin and Kate leaped up from behind the sand dune and grabbed my arm.

I tried to sound aloof.

"Only because I got bored of waiting for you to discover where I was," I said. "I don't suppose you've seen my parents, have you? I fancy lemonade."

Tamsin looked at me with all the superiority of her eleven years. "I guess they are where you left them," she said. "Over by the steps."

She grabbed my arm and pulled me to the top of the dune. "They were just over . . ."

Tamsin stopped dead and her mouth dropped open. And in that instant I wanted to die.

Down on the sands, my mother was shrieking at my father, stamping her foot and hurling cups and flasks and plastic boxes from our picnic hamper all over the sand.

Dad put his arms out as if to hug her but she thrust him away.

"You fool! You total, complete imbecile!"

Her words carried on the wind, and out of the corner of my eye I could see Tamsin and Kate exchanging wide-eyed glances and pulling faces at one another.

And then, while I stood rooted to the spot, trying to brush the sand out of my eyes, I saw my mother lift her hand.

And she slapped Dad.

Right across the face.

Twice. Once with her left hand and once with her right.

I saw Dad stagger back, and then put his hand to his cheek. I heard Tamsin and Kate gasp in horror. Then Mum turned and began running. She was running directly towards us and she was howling like an animal in pain.

My heart was pounding so fast that I thought I might collapse. "Rehearsing," I said, swallowing hard and turning to face my friends. "She's got this amazing part in . . ."

"She's an actress?" Kate was staring wide-eyed at the unfolding scene.

"Really?" Tamsin gasped.

"Film star," I corrected her. "On location. They start

filming tomorrow. And look – you'd better go; if you interrupt her flow, she will go mad. She's very temperamental."

She was getting nearer, with Dad hard on her heels, calling and waving his arms.

"Julia, love, come back. It's OK. Julie! Julie!"

I took a deep breath and tried to smile.

"It's a dead dramatic film, about love and passion and . . ."

I struggled to think of the right word.

". . . pent-up emotion," I finished.

Tamsin and Kate looked at one another and I offered up a silent prayer.

"Will you be here tomorrow?" Tamsin asked. "So we can get her autograph? Please?"

It was that final appeal that made me realise I was on to a winner. "Sure you can!" I nodded. "About half past two?"

I knew we'd be on the way back to Kettleborough long before then.

"Just go now, OK?"

And they went.

That was the first time I realised how easy it is to lie. But it wasn't the last.

"Casualty" is over and I realise I'm shaking. I haven't a clue what happened to the madwoman in the programme and I can only remember bits of what happened with Mum and Dad after that day on the beach. I haven't thought about it in a long time, but when I try, I can remember getting into the car and Mum crying a lot, and saying she was sorry, and then Dad hugging her and saying it was all going to be fine. I remember Mum buying me ice cream and a new pair of jeans and saying I wasn't to worry. And I know that Dad had a bruise above his eye and scratch marks on his forehead and when people asked what was wrong, he joked about having an argument with the roof rack when he was packing up to go home.

I never asked Mum why she was so angry with Dad. I don't think in those days I wanted to know. I know I saw them kissing and cuddling the night Simon got home from adventure camp and I was so relieved that things were back to normal, I guess I assumed it had been a one-off row.

I wish.

Joshua's crying. Good. I'll go and get him and that will make me stop thinking about Mum. You know, I guess that must have been the start of her going crazy, that day on the beach in Norfolk, five whole years ago. So why didn't Dad do something? Take her to the doctor and get pills or something. Why did he keep making excuses? And why did he let her treat him like that?

OK, Josh, I'm coming. Hang on.

He must have known something was wrong. I mean, people don't hurl things about and scream and shout if they're normal.

Only – I do.

But that's when people get to me.

Maybe that was how Mum felt. Maybe she just felt like

bursting into a thousand pieces like I do sometimes. Maybe she had things going on inside her head and didn't know how to tell anyone about them.

But now Mum's in hospital because she's gone doolally.

Does that mean that I'll end up there one day? If I don't tell someone what goes on in my mind, will that happen to me?

I blot out the thought and stomp upstairs and into the nursery.

Josh is purple in the face, screaming with rage. And he's soaking wet; I mean drenched. He looks like he's been yelling for ages but he can't have been because I would have heard him.

I'm about to unbutton his Babygro when the front door slams.

"Georgie! We're . . . !"

"Ssssh!"

The Carters! They can't be back already. They've hardly been gone any time. I glance at my watch. It's ten o'clock. I can't believe it.

"Oh dear, dear, dear, what is going on?"

Mrs Carter flies into the room on a cloud of perfume and alcohol.

"Joshy Woshy darling, what's the matter? Come to Mummy!"

She grabs Joshua from my arms and clutches him to her. He carries on yelling like a thing possessed.

"He's a bit wet . . ." I start, but she's already spotted the damp patch spreading across her sequinned top and is looking horrified.

"Georgie, he's soaking! And his face is burning hot! What's been going on!"

I lean my head slightly to one side and look anxious.

"I think he had a bad dream, Mrs Carter," I say, raising my voice above Joshua's persistent shrieks. "I thought it was more important to pacify him than to upset him more by changing his nappy."

Mrs Carter nods. "Right," she says. "Well, off you go, Georgie. I'll deal with Joshua now. Oh, and ask my husband for your money on your way out."

"Thanks, Mrs Carter," I say. "And do let me know when you need me again."

"Mmm," she murmurs, stripping Joshua's clothes off him.

But I know she won't.

Some mothers are so over the top.

I'm shattered. All I want to do is go to bed and sleep but there's this stupid History essay to do. Maybe I'll set the alarm and do it in the morning. That would be best.

I can hear Dad's voice on the phone in the study as I hang up my jacket.

"Of course, yes, I'll see you tomorrow."

He puts the phone down and spins round in his swivel chair as I walk into the room.

"Oh! Georgie! You're back! Baby-sitting go all right?"

"Fine!" I lie. "Was that Mum?" I gesture to the phone.

"What? Oh, yes, yes. Fine. Great. Really good. Fancy a cup of tea?"

I shake my head. I don't want to give Dad the chance to start getting all depressed and tearful again. "I'm wrecked," I say. "I'm going to bed. See you in the morning."

"Right," he says. "Oh, and Georgie – you will look in on Mum again after school tomorrow, won't you?"

Oh no. No way.

"It's your turn, Dad – we agreed: I do one day, you do the next. Besides, you just promised her that you would see her."

He stares at me blankly and then snaps his fingers. "Ah, yes – bit of a problem there. It wasn't till I'd put the phone down that I remembered. I've got a sales meeting."

"So go when it's finished."

He shakes his head.

"I've got to take a couple of our reps out for dinner – won't be back till late. Sorry, love."

Tough.

"Look, Dad, you've got to go. You need to see what she's like. I just don't think you've taken on board how bad she is. Go in the morning on your way to work, for heaven's sake."

He gets up and comes over to the door.

"I can't do that, Georgie, not when I've got to conduct a meeting. I'd be fit for nothing. Seeing her in that place – it cuts me up. I can't do it."

"And I suppose you think I enjoy it? God, Dad – I'm sick of hearing about the things you two can't do! Mum says she can't come home, you say you can't go and see her . . ."

Dad puts a hand on my shoulder but I jerk myself out of the way.

"It's only for tomorrow, love. I just . . ."

"Oh yes? And what about last Monday? And Wednesday? You keep making excuses – you've only seen her twice in the past week!"

Dad walks into the hall and sits down on the bottom stair. "I guess," he says slowly, "it's hard for you to understand."

"Yes, it bloody well is!"

He looks at me. "Don't swear, Georgie."

"Sorry."

Can't he see that swearing is better than hurling things?

He stands up and walks into the kitchen.

"You must try to see things from my point of view – with Mum ill, I'm the only breadwinner and if I don't make a good impression, I might lose the job. Last in, first out – you know the sort of thing."

He drops his eyes and runs his fingers through his hair.

"I know that compared to the jobs that Mum has had in the past, mine is pretty mundane but at least I've got one and I've worked really hard and . . ."

I feel dreadful now. I mean, it wasn't his fault he got made redundant twice in the last four years. He spent months job hunting last year before he landed this one. Mum was always going on at him about making something of his life and I used to tell her that not everyone could be a high-flyer like her and she ought to stop nagging.

And now I'm nagging him just as much.

I go over to him and wrap my arms round his waist.

"It's OK, Dad. I understand. Of course I'll go."

He beams at me and ruffles my hair. "There's my girl," he says. "I knew I could rely on you."

"Only . . ."

"Yes?"

I take a deep breath. "Promise me you will go on Thursday?"

He crosses his arms over his chest. "Cross my heart," he says. "Now can I have my goodnight kiss?"

I lift my face and he kisses my forehead.

"Night, Dad."

"Sweet dreams," he calls as I clatter up the stairs.

I rather hope I won't have any dreams at all.

CHAPTER THREE

WEDNESDAY
morning

I did dream and it wasn't sweet. I dreamed I was visiting Mum at the hospital and the moment I walked in the room, this huge metal door slammed behind me and two nurses, both looking just like Miranda Jenks, jumped out and grabbed my wrists.

"You're staying here," they said.

"That's right," Mum added. "You're being locked up for driving me crazy."

"And trashing your bedroom," said Miranda Number One.

"And being horrible to your father," added Miranda Number Two.

"NO!" I screamed, fighting to get away.

I pummelled Miranda Number One with my fists.

"You're just like your mother!" spat the other Miranda.

"Mad! Just like me," grinned Mum and her lip was bleeding and she was waving a thermos flask over her head.

I kicked them all and ran to the window, forcing it open. But outside there were rows of kids all leering up at me. Liam and Jamie were at the front with the two girls from Norfolk, and the whole crowd was shouting at me.

"Crazy! Crazy! Raving mad!"

Then Mum burst into tears and lay down on the floor and began kicking her legs in the air and turning purple in the face. And one of the Mirandas threw a blanket over my head and I could hardly breathe and I cried and kicked and screamed as well.

And then I woke up with the duvet smothering me.

I didn't get back to sleep for ages and then I slept right through my alarm, which is why I have now missed the school bus and am belting along the road, praying that I'll make it to school before Registration. There's precious little chance of that happening, which means Mrs Kingham will give me a mouthful and probably a detention – and that's before she discovers I haven't done my History homework and that my Geography book is in the gutter in the High Street. Life can be very unfair.

You would have thought that Dad would have guessed I was still asleep when he was able to get into the bathroom at the first attempt, and come to wake me up, but if you ask me he was so wrapped up in this meeting today that he'd forgotten I existed. By the time I flew downstairs, throwing my clothes on as I went, he was standing in front of the hall mirror, spruced up like a dog's dinner. He had a new suit and everything and he really looked quite good, sort of more erect and up for it than usual.

I asked for a lift but he said he didn't have time – he was picking someone up and couldn't afford to be late. Honestly, where are parents when you really need them?

I can't get that dream out of my head. I know it's silly – obviously nothing like that is going to happen. But that bit when they said I was getting just like Mum – well, it's true. I don't hit people but I do trash things and I feel angry all the time and I can't think straight or concentrate properly. Maybe it's a hereditary illness and it's just a matter of time before I go totally insane. Maybe Simon has escaped it because he's a boy and it only affects the female line. I've read about diseases that do that.

I'm panting for breath but somehow I don't think the pain in my chest is just down to running so fast. I might as well stop, anyway. I'll never make it now. In fact, I might just as well turn round and go home and pretend I'm ill. It's double Maths first period and the thought of that is enough to make anyone sick. And I guess if I don't turn up, Amber will think I'm really ill, and be extra nice to me.

I can feel a lovely warm orange cloud coming down over my head, a sort of tropical island cloud. I close my eyes and imagine what it would be like to be lying in a hammock between two palm trees, swaying in a breeze and eating the largest ice-cream sundae in the world. There's no one else on the island, no one to decide whether I'm crazy or sane. Just me, drifting on my orange cloud . . .

Suddenly the dream is shattered amid manic hooting and honking. I open my eyes, and there's a screech of tyres and a cloud of dust and this battered old VW Beetle mounts the kerb, narrowly missing a lamppost.

"Georgina! Morning! Hop in!"

It's her. Flavia Mott. The dotty woman from next door.

I shake myself and stare. She is wearing a baggy sweater in multi-coloured stripes, a pair of lime green trousers and a battered felt hat. Dress sense this woman does not have.

"Quick, quick!" she says.

"I'm on my way to school," I murmur, hitching my school bag up my shoulder and trying to look as if the idea of taking a sickie never crossed my mind.

"Well, clearly," she grins. "And at this rate, you're not likely to get there in a month of Sundays. In!"

And I get in.

Don't ask me why. It just sort of happened.

"Seat belt," she orders, ramming at the gear lever. "With my driving, you'll need it!"

The car lurches backwards. "Silly me, that's reverse!" she giggles, changing gear again – and then the car coughs a lot and judders back on to the road.

"Which school?" she asks, sticking out her tongue at a

motorist who has just waved two fingers at her and yelled something about women drivers. "I haven't got to grips with the local seats of academe yet!"

"Wheatley Hill High," I say. "But honestly, you don't have to . . ."

"I know I don't *have* to," she says. "I happen to want to. I only do things I want to do. It's part of my philosophy."

"Lucky you."

What am I on? Why am I talking to her like this?

"Not luck, dear – just single-minded stubbornness and a lifetime of experience. Left or right?"

She's jammed on the brakes as the traffic lights turn red.

"Right, then left by the church and fourth on the right," I say.

She nods and peers through the windscreen. I try to think of something intelligent to say and fail.

Suddenly there's this awful wail right behind my left ear and I almost jump out of my skin.

"Harry! Stop that nonsense this instant!"

Flavia scowls into the driving mirror. The wail carries on and I turn round.

It's a cat. A pure white, fluffy cat with eyes like lasers, sitting in a wicker basket on the back seat. It has one paw stuck through the mesh door and looks decidedly bad-tempered.

"Thought I'd get the feline into the new house before the furniture van arrives," she says. "Very temperamental, cats."

"So Harry is a cat," I hear myself say as we hurtle away from the traffic lights. "I thought he was your husband."

She roars with laughter and crunches the gears.

"Good grief, no!" she chortles. "I gave up on men decades ago. And it's Ari, dear."

"Pardon?"

"The cat. Ari. Short for Aristippus."

She turns and grins at me and narrowly misses a man on a bicycle.

"Very apt for a cat, I thought."

She clearly expects me to comment.

"Is it from *The Aristocats*?" I ask, noting with some relief that we are only two blocks away from school.

"Good guess," she says, "but no. Aristippus was a hedonist. And all cats are hedonists. So you see – good name."

She brakes sharply and pulls up outside school.

"Here we are, then!" she says, leaning across me and opening the door. "Off you go – oh, and look up hedonist in the dictionary. It's spelt just as it sounds. You clearly haven't a clue what I'm on about! See you later. *Ciao!*"

And with that, she roars off, her exhaust backfiring as she disappears down the road.

She's got a nerve. Implying that I'm thick just because she can't talk in plain English.

But it was kind of her to give me a lift. Two minutes later, and I'd have been in deep trouble. I wouldn't have skived off really. Being home alone means you end up thinking too much, and that's not a very good idea right now.

I catch up with the tail end of a crowd of Year Nines piling through the double doors, just as the Registration bell rings. As I push through to my locker, I fumble in my bag for a pen.

HEDONIST, I scribble on the palm of my hand in capital letters. I'll look it up later. That'll show her.

She's weird, Flavia – and bossy. But not in a scary kind of way. Not like some people I could mention.

I've just realised. I haven't thought about Mum since Flavia picked me up.

What's more, the horrid dream is fading. I don't feel quite so scared any more.

And that's quite something for me.

"Georgie! What happened? You weren't on the bus. I was worried."

Amber is waiting for me when I get to the classroom.

"I got a lift from the woman next door," I tell her, dumping my school bag on the table.

"You what? There is no woman next door to you."

"There is now," I say. "She's moving in today. So it looks like your plan is a non-starter."

She frowns at me. "What plan?"

"The Wilderness, remember? Big-time seduction in the laurel bushes?"

She waves a hand airily. "Oh that," she replies, breaking

into a broad grin. "After last night, I think I can manage quite nicely without the help of any shrubbery, thank you."

She closes her eyes in a dreamy sort of way. "You can't imagine how amazing it was," she sighs.

"So tell me," I reply, knowing she will anyway.

"Well," she begins, "we went to the cinema and then out for a coffee and then, on the way home, he kissed me."

This is not earth-shattering news. Every male that Amber looks at appears to end up slobbering all over her. I reckon it's the chest that does it.

"And?"

"And it was like the world stopped and the whole meaning of existence fell into place and I knew I could do anything, become anyone, as long as Nick and me were together."

"That's nice," I say. "What's a hedonist?"

She looks miffed at being interrupted in mid-flow.

"What?"

"Hedonist," I repeat. "What does it mean?"

"Haven't a clue," she says. "Why do you – oh no! Georgie – it's not – I mean, you haven't heard anything?"

I'm trying to work out what on earth she's talking about when Mrs Kingham strides into the room and slams a pile of books on her desk.

"Settle down, Eleven–K! This is a classroom, not a monkey enclosure!"

She thinks she's so witty, that woman.

"The tests," whispers Amber. "Have you heard something?"

Suddenly it clicks. After what I told her about having to have tests, I guess she thinks hedonist is some kind of illness. I put my finger to my lips in a conspiratorial manner and lean towards her.

"I'll tell you later," I say. "When we are alone."

And when I've managed to think up something quite heart-rending but yet totally convincing.

Which could take some time.

It's on days like today that I'm quite pleased that Amber is one of those good at everything types of people. She's in the top set for most subjects, so we don't get to do many lessons together, which means she can't keep pestering me for information. But if I haven't thought up a watertight story by lunch break, I'm in big trouble.

I'm on my way to French, running through a list of all known illnesses that don't require visible symptoms, when Caitlin and Rebecca cruise up, arms linked and both wearing the sort of expressions that you just know mean trouble.

"So," says Caitlin, "give us the low-down on this party of yours."

"The one we haven't had an invitation for – yet," adds Rebecca.

"The one that no one has had an invitation for," smirks Caitlin. "Despite the fact that your birthday is next week."

"Unless, of course," adds Rebecca, "there isn't going to be a party, on account of you not having enough friends to fill a shoebox, never mind The Purple Pine Tree."

Oh sugar. I forgot. About a month ago, when this new club opened in an old shoe factory in town, I said that my mum was going to arrange for me to have my birthday party there. The only way under eighteens can get in is to have a private party, so of course everyone was dead keen on the idea. Trouble is, Mum never said it and I'm about to get caught out.

"Oh puh-leese!" I say, thinking on my feet. "With the reputation that place is getting? Give me credit for a bit of taste!"

I don't imagine for one moment that they will fall for that one, but they hesitate and glance at one another just long enough for me to quicken my pace and get to the language laboratory ahead of them. For once, God is on my side and Mrs Tucker is already at her desk. She is one of the nicest teachers in the whole school and she likes me, which is convenient.

"Please, Mrs Tucker," I say, "I've had real problems with the last paragraph of our French translation."

This is largely because I haven't even opened the book yet, but she's not to know that and while she gets all excited about subjunctives and past participles, Caitlin and Rebecca have no choice but to sit down and shut up.

One to me. For now.

It's no good. When I see my mother this afternoon, I'm

going have to pin her down and make her talk about my birthday. She could write me a cheque, always assuming she still remembers how to hold a pen. Then I can organise my own birthday.

That's cool. That's what I'll do.

Sorted.

I'm quite clever sometimes. Pity it never surfaces in French though.

I'm out of favour with everyone today. Mrs Kingham's given me detention because of the non-appearance of the History essay, I've got to pay for the lost Geography book and now I've got C-minus for last week's English homework.

"I really don't know what has got into you, Georgina!" Mrs Lightbody said when she handed it back. "Two years ago, I saw you as a pupil of great potential. Now it seems you don't know the meaning of hard work. Is something bothering you? Is there a reason for this change in attitude?"

I didn't answer, of course. What would be the point? How do you explain that when you shut down your brain in order to stop thinking about the horrible things that are happening, you can't suddenly zap it into action again just because some teacher wants a quick analysis of *The Turn of the Screw*. When you spend half your life wrapped in clouds, some of it seeps into your head and makes you vague and sort of switched off. I can't even explain it to myself so what would be the point of trying to explain it to them?

Come to think of it, what's the point of anything right now?

Amber collars me on the way to the last lesson of the morning. I can see that concerned and caring expression and decide to get in first.

"So go on!" I cry, trying to sound really enthusiastic and interested, "tell me about Nick. Is he really keen?"

She goes all soft and gooey and squeezes my arm.

"He's besotted!" she says with a grin. "He says I'm the most amazing thing that has ever happened to him."

She leans towards me. "But anyway, tell me about . . ."

"And the kiss?" I interject hurriedly, as we head up the stairs. "Tell me about the kiss."

I have to keep her talking.

"I've never been kissed, not properly," I add, knowing that this revelation will make her even more eager to spill the beans.

"What? Never?" She sounds as astonished as if I had admitted to never taking a shower.

I shake my head. "So go on."

"Well," she says, with a long, lingering sigh. "It was like nothing I've ever known before. His lips just moulded with mine and my knees turned to jelly – no, really they did – and we stood there, locked in this embrace for what seemed like hours. And then . . ."

She hesitates. We've another flight of stairs to do yet, so I urge her on.

"Yes?"

"He did it."

Never mind next lesson. I stop dead in my tracks.

"WHAT? You mean, It-it? Right there, in the street?"

Amber looks at me askance. "Not IT, stupid. Tongues. Proper French kissing. For ages. I'd never done that before either," she admits, dropping her voice in embarrassment.

"Wow!" I can't think of anything more meaningful to say but it seems sufficient for Amber.

She nods her head. "I feel like I'm really a woman now," she says. "Kind of rounded and complete. I'm going to get a balcony bra after school."

She pushes open the door of the classroom.

"You know," she says suddenly, turning to face me, "that's what you need."

"A balcony bra?"

A bust would be a good start.

"No, idiot," she grins. "A guy. A relationship."

She narrows her eyes and looks at me in a very meaningful manner.

"You know, love and intimacy are very therapeutic," she adds. "I read about it in this book – love can cure anything."

She puts great emphasis on the word "cure" and alarm bells start ringing in my head. Fortunately I see a way out almost at once.

"Oh look – there's Nick now," I say, nudging her arm. "You'd better go and grab the seat next to him before Caitlin gets there."

Amber's face clouds. "You don't think they still fancy one another, do you?"

I shrug. "Doubt it," I say. "But knowing Caitlin Maltby, I wouldn't take any chances, if I were you."

She's gone before I've finished the sentence and by the time Mr Rowe arrives, she's Velcroed herself to Nick's left arm.

I'm relieved but I know my luck has to run out some time.

And I think it might be soon.

I'm not listening to all this. I don't see the point of these stupid lessons anyway. Personal and Social Education, they're called, and they are supposed to give you an insight to what Mr Rowe calls the wider world of work and citizenship. Today it's all about mental health and care in the community and this I do not need.

"Of course, we have to acknowledge that there is still a lot of prejudice about mental illness," he says. "Some people think that the mentally sick should be cared for in the community and others believe they should be locked away in hospitals where they cannot be a danger to anyone."

I can see that metal door from the dream slamming behind me.

"Now, Eleven–K, I'd like us to think about this whole important issue and I shall expect you all to contribute to the discussion . . ."

It's a black cloud this time and those are the bad ones. It's hovering above my head and I try to ignore it. You don't climb on black clouds and let them whisk you away; you avoid them like the plague.

". . . must remember that mental illness takes many forms . . ."

The cloud is expanding; it's blotting out the light and making the air smell stale. I rest my head on my hands and stare down at my book. That's one advantage of really long hair; it acts as a curtain that stops other people seeing your face.

". . . almost one in four adults will suffer from some sort of psychiatric illness during their lifetimes . . ."

The cloud is getting nearer. It's sitting on top of my head, and my temples are throbbing.

". . . depression, anxiety, panic attacks, schizophrenia are all forms . . ."

I wish he would shut up. What does he know about it anyway? I saw his eyes darting back and forth to the book on his desk. He's just reading the stuff out, like Mrs Plastow does in RE.

". . . of course, some mentally ill people have to be hospitalised, if they become out of control or . . ."

The black cloud drops like a stone right over me. Clouds are not meant to be heavy but this one is. The weight of it on my chest is stopping me from breathing properly.

"*She's out of control, I can't cope.*"

I can hear Dad's voice, shaky and cracking, on the telephone. And suddenly, as if a video is playing in front of my eyes, I see it all over again.

She'd never been that bad before. She'd thrown the occasional saucepan lid, and once she tipped a glass of wine over Dad's head. But that Sunday . . .

I didn't understand it then and I don't understand it now. It had been a good day, the best in ages. Simon was home for the weekend, and Mum had been really cheerful. She hadn't wandered about in her dressing-gown all morning, drinking coffee and eating Liquorice Allsorts, which was what she'd done every weekend for weeks before. She had got dressed and spent hours cooking this huge Sunday lunch with all the trimmings. We'd had roast beef with roast potatoes and three vegetables and home-made Yorkshire pudding, really crispy round the edges. She had even made a proper trifle, with loads of sherry and lashings of whipped cream. Simon had been telling us stories about the people he'd met at uni and we'd had a real laugh, all four of us.

And then I messed up. I can hear myself now.

"Wow, Mum," I said, "that was great! I was getting sick of pizzas and instant dinners – thought your brain had forgotten how to cook!"

It was meant to be a joke, honestly.

She looked at me.

"So you're implying that I'm not a proper mother, are you?"

"I didn't mean . . ."

"So what did you mean?" she yelled. "Just because I don't slave over a cooker morning, noon and night, I'm not worth having, is that it? WELL, IS IT?"

She slammed her fist on to the table and her glass of red wine juddered and then fell over, spilling its contents all over Simon's lap.

"Damn!" he shouted. "These jeans were clean on, Mum!"

Dad opened his mouth and then shut it again and began pushing trifle round and round his plate.

"Now look what you've done!" Mum yelled at me. And with that she stormed out of the dining-room and into the kitchen. Dad swallowed and stared after her. Simon kept mopping the wine with his table napkin. I just kept my head down.

Within a minute Mum was back with her arms full.

"Right," she said. "Georgie, washing powder!"

She hurled a carton of Bold Non-Bio at me. The top was open and white powder scattered all over the lunch table.

"You can wash Simon's jeans, since you caused all this!"

"But . . ."

"And while you're at it, cook books!" She flung a couple of Delia Smiths at me, knocking over the water jug as she did so. "You're so particular – cook your own food in future!"

At last Dad said something. "Julia, love, it's all right, just calm down and . . ."

"Oh, calm down, is it?" Mum shrieked, with tears now coursing down her cheeks. "Do you have the first idea of what it's like? Do you? Of course you don't! None of you do!"

By now she was sobbing uncontrollably. "Georgie says I never cook proper food . . ."

"Mum, that's crazy!" I pleaded. "I didn't mean . . ."

"Oh, so I'm crazy now, am I?" Mum shouted. "Well, if I am, it's you that's made me that way!"

And then it happened. She began tearing at her hair as if she wanted to pull it out in handfuls. Then she dropped to her knees and began beating the floor with her fists, wailing and howling in the most terrifying way.

"Mum!" Simon jumped to his feet. "Stop it, please! Get a grip!"

He bent down and tried to get her to stand up. She stopped crying and stared at him.

"You too?" she whispered. "You're against me as well?"

"Of course not," Simon began, but Mum just leaped to her feet, crashed out into the hall and out of the front door.

It slammed violently behind her.

"Julia! Come back!" Dad yelled, rushing after her and yanking open the door, with Simon and me hard on his heels.

She was standing there. In the middle of the road.

Crying and shaking and pulling at her hair.

A car honked at her and weaved its way past, and I could see the occupants staring, open-mouthed, as Dad grabbed Mum's arm and dragged her, screaming and crying, back into the house.

"I'm sorry, Mum," I whispered, taking her hand.

But that just made her cry all the more.

Dad got her to bed and told us that she'd be fine by the morning. "It's her hormones," he said. "Change of life."

But the next day she wasn't better. She didn't get up and she didn't speak. She just lay in bed with her face to the wall and when I took her a cup of tea she was chewing the flesh on the back of her hand and wimpering like a wounded puppy. It was horrible.

"Go to school," Dad said. "She'll be great by teatime."

Simon left for university after breakfast and didn't say when he'd be coming again. When I got home from school, Dad was in the hallway.

"Thank goodness you're home, Georgie," he stammered. "It's Mum. She's in the cupboard and she won't come out."

OK, so it sounds funny now but it wasn't. Mum had shut herself in the walk-in wardrobe and through the slatted panels I could see her sitting, rocking backwards and forwards, crying and shaking like a leaf. Her eyes were red and swollen and her face was as white as a ghost. Just looking at her scared me rigid.

"You talk to her, Georgie," Dad pleaded. "She'll listen to you."

Which was a pretty daft thing to say, seeing as how Mum doesn't like me much. I did try, though. She didn't listen; she just went on rocking.

That's when Dad phoned the doctor. And at six o'clock, when most mums would be cooking tea, the doctor came and he and Dad took Mum to St Gregory's. And she didn't even kiss me goodbye.

"Georgina Linnington!"

Mr Rowe is standing over me, smelling of cheap aftershave and stale tobacco.

"Could you stop muttering to yourself and read the passage on page forty-five? Out loud, so we can all hear."

His lip curls in a sarcastic sneer and I can hear everyone smothering their giggles.

The black cloud is crushing me.

"Do I have to, sir?" I try to sound ingratiating. "Can't someone else do it?"

"No, Georgie, they cannot. Now come along, we don't have all day."

His finger stabs at the page. It's headed "Mental Health in Britain today – are we all mad?"

I can't do this. My throat is closing up and I can taste the bile at the back of my mouth.

"Actually, I don't feel too well, sir." That usually works.

"How convenient! This is presumably the same illness

that stopped you writing my essay last week, and made you late for class on Monday, eh?"

It's not fair.

I won't do it.

"I'm waiting, Georgina!"

The black cloud has sucked me right into its centre.

"Well, stuff you!" I pick up the book and fling it across the room. "You've got a long wait, that's all I can say!"

You can hear the huge intake of breath as everyone in class gasps in astonishment.

"Pick that book up this very instant!"

Mr Rowe is apoplectic with rage. It's hard to move with a dead-weight on your chest but I stumble my way between the tables. I trip over Liam's school bag and kick it out of the way. I reach the book, bend down, pick it up. Rip the pages, hurl it towards Mr Rowe, turn to the door.

"It's not her fault, sir, honestly it's not! She's ill!" I can hear Amber's pleading tone as I hurl myself into the corridor. "Really, sir, she is!"

As the door slams behind me, and I run through the main hall, down the stairs and into the girls' toilets, I realise that Amber really believes my lie.

What is more, she is prepared to stand up for me against the grumpiest, most despised teacher in the whole school.

I should be feeling pretty chuffed, but I'm not. It is just dawning on me what I've done. I can't kid myself any longer. I'm going insane and I've never been so scared in all my life.

I have to get away from here. OK, so in the long run, it won't help, but frankly all I'm concerned about right now is putting a bit of space between me and Mr Rowe. There's only about ten minutes to go until the lunch bell rings and then all hell will be let loose.

Gingerly I push open the cubicle door. There's no one around.

Automatically I go to wash my hands, and that's when I see the writing, smudged and blotchy by now, on my left hand.

HEDONIST.

I wonder what it really does mean? Amber obviously thought it was someone suffering from an awful illness, but it won't be that, because you wouldn't name a cat after some invalid. Not that it matters, of course. It's not like finding out was homework. But still, I'd like to know, if only to stop Flavia being so smug.

I peer out into the corridor. Apart from a couple of Year Sevens sticking paintings on the wall, the coast is clear. I sprint down the corridor, through the double doors and into the staff carpark. I can't afford being seen from any of the windows, so I crouch down and shuffle past the building and then scoot for the gates.

It's raining and my jacket is still on the back of my chair in the classroom; what's more my money is in the pocket which means I can't even catch the bus. And I can't turn left to walk home because that would mean going past the junior playground and the canteen and then the Art block and someone would be certain to see me. So I cross the road and belt down Lilac Crescent, not slowing down until I'm round the bend and almost in Argyll Street.

And there it is, straight ahead. Argyll Street branch library. Libraries are dry and libraries have dictionaries. They also have huge bookshelves to hide behind.

And right now, hiding is about all I am fit for.

They've got some dead good dictionaries in this place. The one we've got at home is ancient, with pages missing and the tiniest print that you have to squint at to be able to read it. But here they've got huge ones with pictures and maps and diagrams.

I've only just got to H. I got waylaid at G, with pictures of giraffes and ginseng (which Mum took to make her feel laid back and which clearly didn't work) and a ginkgo tree (she took that too, because she said it would help the circulation to her brain – some hope). Anyway, I'm at H now.

Hedgehog, hedgerow, hedge sparrow . . .

Got it!

Hedonist – follower of hedonism.

Oh terrific.

No wait. Here it is.

Hedonism – a devotion, especially a self-indulgent one, to pleasure and happiness as a way of life; a doctrine that holds that pleasure is the highest good.

What?

I read it again and then I get it. This Aristippus person thought that being happy and enjoying life was all that mattered. And cats are like that. So Flavia called the cat Aristippus.

That's clever, that is. Especially as she chose a guy whose name ended in Puss. I mean, loads of people would call their cat Tiddles or Cuddles or something equally dumb, but not Flavia. I reckon she's the sort of person who wouldn't do anything that was ordinary or boring.

I'd like to be like that.

I flick through the dictionary, wondering whether she will be impressed when I tell her I know what a hedonist is. You'd never have thought there were so many words in the English language. Not to mention so many totally weird ones.

And then I have an idea.

I can feel myself grinning and I slide down on to the floor, stick my legs out in front of me and begin reading.

I guess I would have still been sitting there now if the librarian hadn't come up to me and asked if I had found what I needed.

"It's nearly two o'clock, dear," she said. "You'll be late for Registration if you don't hurry up."

So I left. But I'm not going back to school. I can't face it, not today. I know I'm going to be in trouble but if I stay out of it for a bit, maybe Amber will convince them that

I'm under enormous stress, and they'll be all caring and concerned and I'll get away with it.

You never know, it might work.

I suppose I've got to go to see Mum now. I don't see why. I haven't got anything new to say to her, and besides, I won't dare open my mouth in case I talk about something else that sends her off into a frenzy.

But I have to go. I promised Dad. But I don't want to.

"I only do things I want to do. It's part of my philosophy."

Suddenly Flavia's words are echoing through my head, as clearly as if she was standing right beside me.

Which of course was all very easy for her to say because she's ancient and can do whatever she wants. When you're my age, you have to do what you're told to do.

Only I don't see why. Mum scares me, she makes me have bad dreams and I'm pretty sure she doesn't want me there anyway.

I won't go.

No one can make me.

I'm nearly sixteen, for heaven's sake.

Which reminds me about the birthday and the cheque I want from Mum.

Clearly Dad is going to be as good as useless over it all, so I guess I don't have much choice.

Funnily enough, I'm not sure that I want a party any more. I mean, I did, way back when Mum first talked about it. But now I can't really be bothered. If it wasn't for the fact of losing face with Rebecca, Caitlin and Emily and all that lot, I'd give the whole thing a miss.

I haven't even got a boyfriend, and everyone else will be with someone and it'll be totally dire.

But not as dire as letting them all find out that I was lying. Not as dire as doing nothing.

I guess I have to go to see Mum.

I guess I'm just not brave enough not to.

"Want a hot chocolate while you wait?"

I look up from the latest edition of *Hello!* magazine into the most amazing pair of green eyes you have ever seen.

"Wha . . . ?"

It's not easy to speak when the dishiest guy in the universe is standing within three centimetres of your left shoulder.

"Hot chocolate," he says. "It's pretty good – not machine stuff."

"Thanks."

He wanders over to the table in the corner and starts pouring from a chrome vacuum flask. He has this gorgeous sandy-coloured hair and a really tight little bum. Dead sexy.

"They don't let me do much round here," he calls over his shoulder, "except chat to the visitors and do the hot drinks."

He brings two polystyrene cups and puts them on the coffee table beside me.

"Are you . . . ?" I hesitate. He clearly isn't a doctor or a nurse – he can't be more than a couple of years older than me.

"Work experience," he says. "I'm Leo."

His handshake is firm and warm and I don't really want to let go.

"So who are you here to see?"

I would rather not tell him but he's sure to find out anyway. "Julia Linnington – she's my mum."

"Really? I didn't know she had a daughter. She's talked about her son – Simon, isn't it?"

I can feel my stomach lurching.

"Yes." The word comes out as a croak.

Obviously Simon is worth chatting about to all and sundry and I'm not. Well, great. I make all this effort to come and she's not ready to see me and now I hear that she doesn't even acknowledge my existence.

I stand up.

"I don't think she's out of her class yet," Leo says. "She's doing Stress Management."

I sling my bag over my shoulder. "Really?" I say sarcastically. "Clearly it's not working."

Leo smiles and I notice that he has the cutest little gap in his front teeth.

"It takes time," he replies easily. "Or at least, that's what they tell me. She's had quite a rough ride apparently."

"But she will get better?"

Leo colours up slightly and looks apologetic. "Look, I'm just here for experience," he says. "What do I know?

Hey – I think I can hear them coming out of the session now."

He moves to the bottom of the staircase and suddenly I know I can't stay. "Well, mention that her daughter dropped by. Always assuming she remembers she's got one!"

I turn and flounce towards the door.

"Hey! Wait!" Leo is beside me in an instant. "She'll be down in a second and she'll be so disappointed to miss you."

"Believe that and you'll believe anything! Thanks for the hot chocolate!"

I stride off down the hall to the main door without a backward glance.

"No, please, don't go!"

Leo's voice is as sexy as his bum and for a moment I'm tempted to stop. But I can hear footsteps on the landing above and I know that I can't face my mother right now, not knowing that she doesn't even talk about me, doesn't miss me one little bit.

So I pretend I haven't heard him, and keep walking.

WEDNESDAY
afternoon

I'm still in a mood as I stomp through the pouring rain up the steps to the front door. I am just ramming my key into the lock when something jumps out from behind the big terracotta pot of pansies that Mum planted and lands on my foot.

It's that cat. Aristippus. His fur is all wet and bedraggled and he's wailing like a banshee, entwining himself between my legs and looking up at me with saucerlike eyes. You are not supposed to let cats out for days after they've moved house but I guess Flavia is too off the wall to think of practical things like that.

To be honest, I'm a bit wary of picking him up because he looks pretty mean to me. But if I leave him and go to get Flavia, he'll probably do a bunk and get even more lost.

I dump my school bag in the hall and Ari follows me in,

tail swishing and nose twitching.

"Oh no, you don't!" I bend down, scoop him up in my arms and march back down the steps and round to Flavia's front door. Surprisingly he just sits there, staring at me and making no attempt to get savage or jump down.

I press the front doorbell with my elbow but nothing happens, so I kneel down, still clutching the cat, push the letterbox flap open with my chin and call.

"Flavia! Mrs – Miss – Mott!"

From inside comes the sound of very loud, and very off-key, singing.

"Fly home, little heart, fly home where you be-long-ong-ong."

I rattle the letterbox frantically and thankfully the singing stops and the large shape of Flavia looms at me through the coloured glass panel in the front door.

She flings open the door and her mouth drops open. "Georgina – and Ari, darling! Where did you come from?"

"I found him on my doorstep," I say, dumping the cat at Flavia's feet. "You are not supposed to let cats out when they've just moved house, you know."

Flavia chuckles. "Believe me, I didn't," she says. "I guess he must have escaped when the removal men left. What a bit of luck that you found him!"

She picks up the cat and grins at me. "Well, come on in – don't just stand there!"

And quite without meaning to I step into the hall.

"Through there," she says, waving a chubby arm. "Second door on the right."

I push open the stripped pine door.

"Wow!"

I can't believe my eyes. This room is amazing. The floor is covered with the brightest rugs you've ever seen and the wall opposite is almost hidden under pictures and wall hangings and bizarre masks and carvings. And everywhere there are piles of books – on bookcases, on the floor, on the big rocking-chair in the far corner, even on the tiled hearth. Big books, paperbacks, picture books – it's like a bookshop on delivery day. She's clearly been trying to get straight – and failing. There's a lopsided shelf nailed precariously to one wall and a lot of trailing wires to table lamps shaped like mermaids and Grecian goddesses.

"Everywhere else is a tip," Flavia says cheerfully, as if this room was straight out of *Homes and Gardens*. "But I can't relax till I have my books and my pictures about me. Carrot cake?"

"Pardon?"

"It's teatime, so cake!" she declares. "Stay there – I'll go and rustle something up."

I've never seen so many books outside a library. I pick the top one off the pile on the rocking-chair.

Handbook for Women Travellers it's called, and it's full of stuff about how to cope with insects in the jungles of Borneo and how to avoid getting ripped off in Bolivia. Given the state of my life, I'm hardly likely to leave Kettleborough, so I rummage around for something more interesting.

After a bit I find this wicked book all about giants and

nymphs and goblins. The pictures are amazing; like something out of a surreal film. I'm so engrossed that I don't hear Flavia coming back into the room.

"Great book, that one, isn't it? I never get tired of looking at it."

I put it down hastily.

"Borrow it, dear," she says with a grin. "You'll love it."

"But it's a kid's book!" I protest, not wanting her to think I'm thick or something.

"Oh dear me, not another one!" She clamps a hand to her forehead.

"Pardon?"

"So many people think that picture books are forbidden after the age of about six," she sighs. "Crazy. I mean, look at this."

She grabs the book, flicks through the pages and stops at a wonderful picture, all sea greens and aquamarine and splashes of lilac, with half-hidden faces in a jungle of leaves.

"Every time you look at that you see something new," she declares. "Let your imagination run riot. Be a kid again. Best therapy in the universe!"

I stare at the picture. She's right. There's a tiny snail falling off a broken flower stem. There's a face peering from a hollow tree-trunk, looking inquisitive but somehow shady, so you know that when you read the words on the opposite page you'll find out he is up to no good.

"Now look," cries Flavia, "come to think of it, we'll eat in the kitchen. Bring the book."

And with that she marches me down the hall and into the kitchen. On the table is a huge cake with thick icing. She takes a knife, cuts two huge wedges and dumps one in front of me.

"Tea? I've only got camomile or Earl Grey, I'm afraid. Which is it to be?"

I don't like to admit that I've never had either.

"Whichever you're having," I say, nibbling at the cake. It is to die for.

"No can do!" Flavia folds her arms and grins at me.

"Pardon?"

Honestly, having a conversation with this woman is worse than trying to get sense out of my mother.

"You must decide," she says, turning on the tap and filling the kettle. "I can't abide people who follow the herd. Now, make a choice."

I shrug. "Camo – thingy," I say.

She laughs. "Good choice," she says, plugging in the kettle. "Very calming – and excellent when you've had a bad day."

"How do you know I've had a bad day?"

She sits down, wraps her arms across her huge bosoms and shrugs. "I didn't – I was just commenting on the properties of the camomile leaf. But now you've said that, I know you have. Tell all!"

She gets up again and pours boiling water on to teabags.

"My mum loves my brother better than . . ."

Dear God, what am I doing? I don't even know the

93

woman. I shove another piece of cake into my mouth and shut up.

"Better than you? I doubt it very much."

Flavia hands me a mug of tea and sits down opposite me.

"She might *like* him better than you right now . . ."

Oh thanks!

". . . but that's not the same as *loving* him better. Have you talked to her about it?"

Well, what can I say? That you can't talk to my mother, because she either sits there in silence or else screams her head off at you? That she's in hospital telling the entire world how wonderful Simon is and not even mentioning the fact that I exist? That Leo says she's complicated – and maybe she won't get better.

"I don't want to talk about it," I say, as a soft yellow cloud wraps itself round me. It's a very warm cloud which might have something to do with the green Aga in the corner of Flavia's kitchen, and I have to fight the urge to close my eyes and simply drift away. Of course, I can't possibly let that happen in someone else's house so I nibble my fingernails and concentrate on the cake.

"Then we won't talk about it!" smiles Flavia. "Now tell me, do you think I should do these walls in lilac or aquamarine?"

"Neither," I murmur. "Egg yolk yellow."

Flavia cocks her head on one side and surveys the walls. "You know," she cries, thumping the table, "I do believe you're right! Splendid idea! Egg yolk yellow it shall be!"

I look at her in total amazement. "I didn't mean – I mean, I was just thinking about something and . . ."

Flavia waves her arm dismissively. "Never justify your intuition!" she cries. "Go with your gut feeling, it's the only way! More cake?"

I shake my head and brush my hands together to get rid of the crumbs – and the ink smudges at the base of my fingers remind me.

"I found out what a hedonist is," I say, thankful for a change of subject. "Someone who is devoted to pleasure and happiness."

"Bravo!" Flavia claps her hands in delight. "So you bothered to look it up? Well done, you!"

"And I found out what . . ." I glance at my other hand. ". . . homonym means."

I struggle over the syllables but I get it out.

Flavia nods. "That's a word that's spelled the same as another one, but has a different meaning, isn't it?" she says. "Like the bow of a ship and bow meaning a ribbon?"

"Oh," I say.

Flavia grins.

"And jongleur?" I urge.

"Wandering minstrel, I think," comments Flavia, brushing crumbs from her lap.

"Oh," I say again.

"You wanted to catch me out," she laughs. "Well, great. Here's one for you." She closes her eyes and puts her finger to her chin. "What is onomatopoeia?"

"Easy!" I cry. I remember that one from the days when Mrs Lightbody used to call me her best English pupil. "It's words that sound like the thing you are describing – you know, like hiss or buzz or splosh!"

"Spot on!" Flavia cries. "What have you been doing all day – reading the dictionary?"

I don't reply even though she's right. Suddenly the game doesn't seem so much fun any more because I'm remembering exactly what I *did* do today and it hits me that come tomorrow morning, I'll be in real trouble at school.

And then there's Amber to sort out and my birthday and when Dad finds out that I didn't hang around to see Mum, he's going to go ballistic.

The cloud gets more inviting by the second and I just want to climb into its centre and go to sleep.

"Georgina? Are you all right?"

Flavia is looking at me in a strange way.

I put on my TV camera smile and face my audience.

"Fine!" I reply. "Just suffering from brain ache after school! Oh – and my friends call me Georgie, by the way."

"And do I count as a friend?" Flavia asks.

"Yes, actually – you do," I reply. And I'm pretty surprised to realise that I'm telling the truth. Which is quite something for me these days.

"Well, thank you," she says as she follows me to the door. "Don't forget the book!"

She thrusts it into my hands. "Bring it back any time,"

she says. "Oh – and tell your mum I'll pop round tomorrow and introduce myself."

"NO!" I spin round to face her. "I mean, you can't. She's away. On business. China. Well, Hong Kong actually."

Lucky save.

"Really? How fascinating? I love the place – lived there for three years back in the Sixties. Where is she staying?"

I swallow hard. How dare she know the place?

"Er – the, um, The Grand," I say. Everywhere has a Grand Hotel. Doesn't it?

Flavia smiles. "Well, for now, I'll just have to settle for saying hi to your father," she went on. "Must be neighbourly, you know."

I'm about to tell her that my father is away too, but even I know she wouldn't swallow that one.

"Thanks for the cake," I say.

"Any time," she replies. "I'm trying a new one tomorrow – you must come and have a nibble."

She grins broadly. "Come again, won't you? It's been lovely," she says. "Really lovely."

I can't help staring at her. She sounds as if she really means it.

CHAPTER FIVE

THURSDAY

That's that, then. I'm on report for the next four weeks. That means that I get a yellow card which I have to take to every lesson. It gets signed by the teachers to say I've behaved. Or not, as the case may be.

I'm pretty fed up about it, to be honest, especially as I thought for a moment, back there in Mr Lamport's study, that I might get away with it.

"It has been suggested to me by one of your friends, Georgina," he intoned, after he'd done the whole bit about damage to school property and lack of self-control, "that you are undergoing various tests in connection with your health. Is this true?"

I shouldn't have hesitated. I should have just kept the story going. Instead, yet again, I blew it.

"Well, sort of."

He was eyeing my file and tapping his pen on the address label and I knew he was planning on ringing my dad. They do that here at Wheatley Hill – Amber says it's to cover themselves, but I reckon they do it out of sheer malice.

"Sort of?" he snorted. "What does that mean? Either you are or you are not."

He didn't give me a chance to interrupt. "And in the absence of any note to the contrary from your parents, I can only conclude that your friend was simply spinning a yarn in a misguided attempt to get you off the hook."

I said nothing. I felt about two centimetres tall, but I wasn't going to let him know that so I just shrugged, yawned and looked out of the window. Big mistake.

"Georgina! I will not tolerate this lackadaisical approach to life! In a few months' time you will be sitting your GCSE examinations and your whole future depends on your getting good grades . . . What do you imagine your parents will feel if you let them down in this manner, just when . . . ?"

I didn't listen after that. I just floated away, out through the window. I didn't even need a cloud this time; I just felt my whole body getting lighter and lighter and then suddenly I wasn't there any more, in his study listening to the same old garbage that he preaches on the first day of every term. Only this time the place I went to wasn't warm and comforting and dreamy; it was black and suffocating and gave me pains in my chest and that closed-up feeling in your tonsils that comes just before you cry really hard. And all I could see in my mind was them. Dad and her. The woman he kissed last night.

If it hadn't been for Amber, I'd never have seen them at all. I mean, it wasn't as if they were daft enough to snog outside the house. But just after I got back from returning Aristippus to his mistress, the phone rang. Well, of course, I didn't answer it, thinking it would be the school trying to reach my dad; but the answerphone cut in and it was Amber.

"Georgie? Are you there?"

I hesitated because I wasn't too sure that I wanted a post-mortem until I'd got my new story straight.

"Georgie! Oh, God, where is she?"

Amber was close to tears. I snatched up the phone.

"I'm here," I panted. "I was in the loo."

"Oh thank goodness! I've been trying to get you all afternoon! Everyone's been going spare!"

Well, I was hardly surprised; after my performance in class it was obvious that she would be itching to tell me what happened next. Amber's great but she loves to think she knows everything about everyone and she doesn't mind telling you to your face what other people might keep behind your back.

"Are you OK?"

I was quite chuffed to hear the genuine concern in her voice.

"Fine," I answered.

"Oh, get real!" she retorted. "You may be safe, but you're certainly not fine. Georgie, what possessed you to do that?"

I didn't reply but Amber was in full flood anyway.

"Now look, you're coming over for supper."

"I'm what?"

"Coming to my place for supper, OK? You said your dad was working late so there's no excuse."

I shook my head, even though she couldn't see me down the phone line. "I can't," I protested. "I've reams of homework to catch up on and . . ."

"Precisely," she interjected. "Look, Georgie, come over and you can crib my coursework. That way, at least you won't be in even more trouble than you are already. And besides, Nick and me have got a plan."

I didn't want another hour of hearing about the amazing Nick but then again, I didn't want three hours of battling with History and Maths, and it was dead cool of Amber to offer. So I went.

Amber lives ten minutes' walk away from me in a house that used to be a vicarage – hence the gravestones next door. I usually cut across the park to get there, but in the evenings you get some dodgy types around, so I walked all the way along Sycamore Avenue, round The Crescent and into Mayflower Drive that way. And that was when I spotted Dad's car, crawling at a snail's pace up The Crescent towards the traffic lights.

I was pretty surprised considering he had told me he

wouldn't be home until eleven at the earliest. I knew he would be really worried if he got home and found me gone (he's so protective of me, which is a pain in public but quite nice at other times), so I stepped off the kerb and was about to wave my arms frantically to attract his attention when I realised he wasn't alone. There was a woman sitting next to him. And needless to say, it wasn't Mum.

I guess I would still have made sure that he saw me had it not been for what happened next. He pulled up as the lights changed to red, turned and put his arm round the woman's shoulders. And then he leaned forward and kissed her.

I wish now that I had run over and hammered my fists on the car window. I wish I had yanked open the passenger door and dragged the creature out and told her where to go. But I didn't. I just stood there, feeling sick. And then the lights changed and he drove off.

I walked to Amber's house in a daze. I couldn't believe what I had just seen. How could Dad be mooning round the house one day, sobbing and wailing because he missed Mum so much – and then, less than twenty-four hours later, be pawing all over another woman? It was obscene.

I could feel myself getting into more and more of a state, so I tried really hard to be rational. I told myself that it could have been the sales rep he was taking to dinner; maybe she had closed a deal and he was just giving her a congratulatory kiss. Except that he had said that he was taking two people out – and what I had seen was no peck on the cheek. It was disgraceful for a middle-aged man with a wife in hospital.

"Georgina! Have you listened to one word that I have said?"

Mr Lamport's roar broke into my thoughts as he thumped his fist on his desk and leaned towards me.

"Yes, sir," I muttered, but of course I hadn't.

"Very well," he says. "I want that essay on my desk . . ."

"Essay, sir?"

"I knew you weren't listening," he snorts. "Five hundred – no, eight hundred – words on self-control by Monday. And what's more, you will bring the money for the damaged book tomorrow, and if anything like this ever happens again . . ." He glared at me, his sentence unfinished. "Go!" he growled.

So I went. I went to Geography and spent most of it on an olive green cloud, and then I went to Art and got shouted at for gazing out of the window instead of drawing three apples and a mouldy-looking tangerine. Now I'm in RE. Amber keeps winking at me across the room and giving me the thumbs-up sign when Mrs Plastow isn't looking.

But then she doesn't have to write an essay on self-control, does she?

While Mrs Plastow rambles on about miracles and turning water into wine, I ask myself how I ever agreed to Amber's plan. Then again, I guess that last night I would have agreed to anything if it stopped me worrying about

Dad and Mum and the future and everything.

The trouble is, Amber has got it into her head that tomorrow night is going to be the solution to all my problems. She was so triumphant when she announced it. We were sitting round her kitchen table, her, me and her mum, Joy, and I was trying to eat the mountain of food that Joy had piled on my plate, which was hard because every time I thought about Dad and that woman, I felt sick. I'm not stupid: I read the newspapers and they are full of stories about men who can't hack it when their wives get ill, so they go off with someone else and start again. And to be fair to Dad, Mum has hardly been sweetness and light this past couple of years.

To make matters worse, Joy kept asking how Mum was, and when she was due back from her trip, and did I think she and Dad would be free for dinner one night?

"Are you OK, Georgie?" Amber's mum asked anxiously when my answers became shorter and shorter. "You haven't eaten much."

"Just not very hungry," I said, dropping my eyes because to my horror they were filling with tears. "Think I've got a cold coming on."

"You'd better not have!" cried Amber, with a broad grin. "Not before tomorrow night, anyway!"

For a moment I forgot Dad.

"Why? What's happening tomorrow?"

Her mum stood up.

"I'll leave you girls to it," she said. "Work calls."

104

She paused, touched my shoulder and then, patting me on the head, left the room.

"So? What are you on about?" I demanded.

"You," declared Amber, "have got a date!"

"A what?"

"It's all organised," she announced. "The way I see it, you need a guy. I told Nick and . . ."

"You told Nick what, exactly?"

"That the reason you were acting all weird and peculiar was because you had health problems and . . ."

She hesitated.

"Go on." I spat the word out through clenched teeth.

". . . and you needed something to take your mind off it all," she continued. "Then I said that I wished you could fall in love, and Nick said he had this mate who hasn't had a girlfriend for months and is desperate for one . . ."

"You didn't?" I just knew what was coming.

Amber nodded eagerly. "It's all organised. Tomorrow night, seven thirty. We're going . . ."

"We are not going anywhere!" I protested. "I mean, this guy is probably a total dork and . . ."

"So? If he is, you don't have to see him again. But he could be the sexiest thing on legs. And besides, have you anything better to do on Friday night?"

Put like that, there wasn't much I could say.

"OK," I agreed.

Amber hugged me. "You know," she declared, "I have a feeling this could be the start of something really big."

I wish. Somehow I don't think a few hours in town with a guy who can't get his own girlfriend is going to transform my life.

But at least it can't make it any worse.

"Still up for it?" Amber mouths across the room now.

I fix a grin on my lips and nod enthusiastically because that's what normal teenagers do when they think about boys.

"You bet," I say. "Can't wait."

She looks dead chuffed.

I'm pleased someone is happy.

At lunch-time I bump into Amber and Nick. Or rather, they bump into me. When people walk along a corridor, gazing into one another's eyes, they tend not to see where they are going.

"You OK?" asks Amber. "I mean, did old Lamppost give you a rollicking?"

I shrug in what I hope is a laid-back manner. "He tried," I say. "But frankly, I think he feels a bit guilty about laying into someone who is – well, you know . . ."

Amber nods. "It's OK – I told Nick. That's when he thought up the idea for tomorrow night."

She gazes at Nick as if he were solely responsible for discovering a cure for cancer and ridding the entire world of the common flea.

"You don't have to talk about it if you don't want to, but . . ."

Amber clearly wants a detailed explanation, and I'm about to make up something when Mr Lamport appears out of the staffroom.

"Ah!" he exclaims and I wait for another outpouring of sarcasm. But it's Amber he's interested in.

"Amber Haig! A word!" He peers short-sightedly at her.

"Perhaps in future you could get your facts right before you open your mouth!"

"Sir?"

Amber looks bewildered. Most people do when confronted by our headmaster. I think he was planted here from another planet.

"So Georgina is in poor health, is she? Undergoing tests at the hospital? So worried that she doesn't know what she's doing, isn't that what you told me?"

Amber throws me a glance and then tilts her chin defiantly. "Yes, sir," she says. "She told me all about it."

Oh whoops.

"She told you?" Mr Lamport's eyebrows shoot upwards and he fixes me with a penetrating stare. "Georgina told you that she . . . ?"

"Yes," continues Amber, "she's being really brave about it and I don't think you should . . ."

"I'm sure she's being brave," says Mr Lamport, glancing in my direction. "It's easy to be brave when there is absolutely nothing wrong with you."

Now I know that the saying about your blood running cold isn't just some made up story. I feel the shiver streaking its way through my whole body. He's found out that I was lying. Worse, he's told Amber. And I haven't had time to think up even the flimsiest of explanations.

"Oh, Georgie!" Amber turns towards me and she doesn't look even mildly annoyed. "So the tests were clear? Oh that's so cool!"

She ignores the fact that the Head is a metre away and flings her arms round me. "I'm so pleased!"

I swallow hard. I can feel Mr Lamport's eyes drilling through my skull and into my brain.

Please, God, just let him walk away. Get him out of earshot and then, just maybe, I can retrieve the situation.

Mr Lamport doesn't move a muscle.

"Georgie?" Amber clearly expects me to say something.

"I think, Georgina, that you owe your friends an explanation, don't you?" Mr Lamport demands. "An explanation of just why you lied in such a blatant manner?"

He turns to Amber. "There were no medical tests, Amber," he says. "Georgina is as fit as you or me."

And with that, he turns and strides down the corridor, his shoes squeaking as he goes.

"I'd better get to footie," mumbles Nick, avoiding my gaze. "See you later, Amb."

He pecks her cheek but she doesn't respond. She is staring at me. There are two spots of colour in the middle of her cheeks.

"It was a lie?" Her voice is high and cracking.

I don't know what to say. What can I say? So I say nothing.

"You let me believe that you were going to . . ." She pauses, her face crumpling. ". . . to die!" she finishes and bursts into tears.

"Amber, don't!"

I reach for her hand but she jerks it away.

"I didn't mean to say it, it just sort of came out!" I cry. "You kept on about how I'd changed and . . ."

"Well, you have!" shouts Amber through her tears. "The old Georgie would never have lied to me. I thought you had cancer, for God's sake. I thought I was going to lose you!"

"Would you – I mean, would it have mattered if you had?"

I can feel my chest getting tighter as I hold my breath.

"What sort of dumb fool question is that?" she shouts back. "You're my best mate, we've been friends since we were six. Why did you pretend to be ill, Georgie? For God's sake, why?"

Because I'm mad. Because I had to say something to stop you thinking I was weird. Because everything's going wrong and I don't think I can cope any longer.

"I thought if I was ill, you wouldn't give up on me," I whisper. "I know it drives you crazy when I – well, when I go off into a world of my own and . . ."

"But that's just you!" protests Amber. "You've done it for years."

"I have?"

"You're a dreamer, Georgie. OK, so it's infuriating and

lately it's been a lot worse, but I wouldn't stop liking you because of that. But I might stop liking someone who tells blatant lies because they don't trust me!"

"Amber, I . . ."

"Do you have any idea what I've been thinking?" she storms. "That night, after you told me, I dreamed you were dead and I was at your funeral watching the coffin going into the ground! It was horrible!"

"I'm sorry, I . . ."

"Yes, well I'm sorry too! Sorry I wasted time trying to think of ways to make you feel better! Sorry I tried to stick up for you!"

I don't know what to say. She's right of course, which makes it worse.

"I thought you'd got a brain tumour!" she cries. "I thought that was why you kept losing it, trashing stuff and going ballistic!"

She looks at me, incomprehension written all over her face. "Why did you do all that?" she demands. "That stupid story about breaking your mum's photo by accident . . ."

"I did," I begin and immediately regret it.

"There you go again!" she shouts. "Lies, lies and more lies! Georgie, your bedroom has the thickest carpet in the universe − glass wouldn't smash on that. You broke them deliberately, I know you did!"

My throat has closed up and I can't speak. She has seen through me. And if she knows that about me, what else does she know?

"Well?" She fixes me with a steely gaze.

I struggle to speak. "Please don't hate me," I say. "You're my best friend."

"Well, I dread to think how you treat your enemies, then!" she retorts.

There's nothing more to be said. She does hate me. I've blown it yet again.

I turn away and begin to walk down the corridor, staring at the floor so that no one will see that I'm crying.

"Georgie?"

I turn round. Amber has her hand on my arm.

"Make me a promise," she says.

"What?" I sniff.

"That you will never, ever lie to me again? About anything? Promise?"

I take a deep breath and nod. "I promise," I say. "Actually, there is one thing I . . ."

At that moment the bell shrills for next period, which I know is meant as a warning to keep my mouth shut.

"What?"

"Can we still have the date tomorrow?" I improvise hastily. "I mean, you still want me to come?"

She nods half-heartedly. "I guess," she replies. "I'll call for you at seven and we'll meet the guys in town."

We start walking to the cafeteria but Amber isn't finished yet. "Why do you keep going ballistic?" she asks. "What is really wrong?"

I take a deep breath.

"I get all muddled in my head," I say. What a jerk! What kind of reply is that?

Amber shakes her head. "Like I said," she adds, "what you need is a passionate love affair. But if you ever lie to me again . . ."

The unfinished sentence hangs in the air.

"I won't," I promise.

It's OK. I mean it. Old lies don't count, though. Do they?

I've been dreading going home. I have to speak to Dad about that woman. I wanted to last night, but even though I did my best to stay awake he wasn't back by gone eleven and I must have fallen asleep. Now I have a horrible feeling that he's going to be confronting me first – there's only one way Mr Lamport could have found out that I was lying, and that was by telephoning Dad. Why can't life be simple – just for a day?

It's even worse than I thought. Dad is waiting for me when I get home. It's only half past five and he's already there, changed out of his work clothes and hovering in the hall.

"Dad, you said you were going to see Mum!" I begin, because someone once said that the best method of defence is attack. "Didn't you go?"

"I'm going in a minute, Georgie," he says, his forehead creased in a frown. "But first – I need to talk to you."

He gestures to me to go into the kitchen. I slouch down at the kitchen table and begin running my fingernail up and down the wood. "Mr Lamport telephoned me today," he begins. "He wanted to know whether it was true that you are ill."

I say nothing. Which as it turns out is just as well.

"Of course, I told him you were fine and that I didn't know what he was talking about. He said he was very pleased to hear that, because Amber had led him to believe you were having tests at the hospital."

I hold my breath and start praying.

He clears his throat. "Georgie, I know you won't like what I'm going to say but . . ."

"What?"

My stomach is doing somersaults of a standard fit for the Olympic games.

"Well, I told him Amber had got it wrong and it was your mum who was having tests."

I'm thinking on my feet. This could be OK. Just as long as he hasn't said too much. "Tests? You actually said tests? Not the bit about her being in St Gregory's and . . ."

He shakes his head. "I didn't tell him the whole story because I didn't know how much you had told Amber," he continues. "I guessed you had taken my advice and tried to tell her, but . . ."

"That's right!" I cried eagerly. "Only I chickened out at the last moment and just said Mum was getting a few tests done."

"That's what I thought!" he said, somewhat triumphantly. "That was good of me, wasn't it? You're pleased?"

He looks so pleading, so desperate for my approval. It makes me feel odd, but frankly right now I'm just relieved that he hasn't spilled the beans about Mum's real state.

"Yes, Dad, that's great. Thanks!"

I get up, assuming the conversation is over, but Dad gestures to me to sit down again.

"I might not have been so ready to go along with your ideas," he begins, "if Mr Lamport had told me about your behaviour earlier on."

He pauses and waits for me to speak. I say nothing.

"He told me that you had misbehaved in class. And that it wasn't the first time. It seems that your grades are dropping and you are not paying attention."

I wait for the inevitable parental enquiry as to my state of mind.

"Frankly, Georgie," he continues, running his fingers through his hair, "I can't cope with any more problems. I have got enough on my plate without you causing more difficulties."

He pauses, chewing his lip as a black cloud hovers above my head. "We've got to pull together, you and I. You must just remember that I depend on you, Georgie. You're all I've got right now."

Oh great. And who is there for me to depend on?

He is in full flood now. "I can't cope with teachers going on and on at me about your schoolwork, asking if there's a reason for your attitude. I couldn't tell him, could I? Not knowing you would make a scene if I did."

I say nothing.

"Georgie, the truth of it is – I can't take any more, OK?"

That does it. The blackness comes down and it's too late to do anything about it.

"Oh terrific!" I shout, sweeping my arm across the table and sending the salt and pepper pots flying to the floor. "You can't take any more! We've got to pull together, have we? And I suppose that means I cook the meals and iron the clothes and run in a bit of homework while you drive around town with some fancy woman, and snog on street corners, is that it? Well, I can't take any more either, OK?"

I stand up, pushing back my chair with such force that it crashes to the floor.

"What . . . ?"

"Oh, Dad, don't try to crawl out of it! I saw you. Last night, with a woman."

He rubs his nose, which is his usual playing-for-time trick. "What were you doing out of the house?"

"Never mind that!" I storm. "You can't deny it, can you? How could you do it, Dad? One minute you're saying that Mum is everything to you and the next you're flirting behind her back! You make me sick!"

"It wasn't like that," he protests. "Jenny's a friend from work. She understands . . ."

"Oh don't give me all that 'she understands me' bit!" I cry. "I saw you kissing her, Dad. And don't you deny it!"

He looks at me sheepishly.

"I'm not denying it," he says. "I did kiss her."

I'm burning hot now. I can feel pins and needles shooting down my arm as though great waves of electricity are surging through my body.

"Oh great! And now I suppose you're going to drive to the hospital and tell Mum how much you love her and miss her and need her, right?"

"I do love her, Georgie, I do miss . . ."

"Hypocrite!" I pick up the newspaper that is lying folded on the dresser and hurl it at him.

"Listen!" he shouts back. "OK, so I kissed Jenny. I couldn't help myself, because she's . . ."

"Oh right! Well, in that case, I couldn't help myself behaving badly in class, OK? I couldn't help getting bad grades and I can't help the fact that I am never, ever going to do another thing for you again! Get it?"

And with that, I storm out of the kitchen, slamming the door as hard as I can, and stomp upstairs to my bedroom.

He calls after me a few times, and then I hear the front door shut and the bleep of his car alarm.

I fling open the window and lean out. "And don't think I'll be cooking supper because I won't. Not today, not ever! You can do it yourself. Get it?"

He looks up swiftly, then scans the street in case anyone has heard me. And then, without a word, he gets into the car and drives off.

The black cloud is all over me now, creeping up my nostrils and making me choke. My throat is sore from shrieking and I want to be sick. I sink to the floor and wrap my arms round my chest and start rocking backwards and forwards.

"Why? Why? Why?"

And then I realise what I'm doing. I'm doing just what she did. Mum. So I am going insane. Whatever was eating away at Mum's mind has got into my brain too, making me yell and scream and shout at people and then act like some backward baby.

I can't bear it. I want to be normal. I want to be like Amber, and Rebecca and Emily and Caitlin. But I'm not. I'm mad. Like her.

I know I'm going to do it, even before I start. I throw my books on the floor and kick them across the room.

"I hate you all!"

I pull my posters off the wardrobe door and rip them into shreds, shouting rude words at the wall as I do so.

But it's not enough. The black cloud is still swamping me and I'll do anything to push it away.

I throw open the side window, seize the book on my bedside table and, without meaning to, fling it as far as I can.

The black cloud starts to lift. I watch the arc that the book makes as it flies through the air.

The cloud divides into little pieces and floats away on the wind. I gaze out of the window at where the book has fallen.

I look straight down into the garden of The Wilderness – into the wide, questioning eyes of Flavia Mott. Flavia

Mott, whose book is lying, crumpled and soiled, at her feet.

"Georgie! Come on down!"

I guess it's only been a millisecond since I hurled her beautiful book into the undergrowth that is her back garden, but it feels like an age. I can't believe I did that. What am I going to say to her?

"Georgie!" she calls again, putting her hand to her eyes to shield them from the setting sun. "I've been having a practice with toffee apples – do come and try one!"

What is she on about? She should be yelling at me but instead, she is smiling and beckoning me down. Slowly I close the window, step over the mess on my bedroom floor and drag myself down the stairs.

I try desperately to think of some explanation for what I've just done. I already know that I am doomed to fail – and frankly, I'm too miserable to care.

"So? What do you think?"

Flavia gestures towards the huge toffee apple she thrust into my hands when she ushered me in from the garden. I take a bite as she scoops Aristippus out of a chair. The cat glares at her indignantly and struts to his basket in the corner of the room.

"The toffee's too chewy, isn't it?" she asks anxiously, flopping down into the now vacant chair. "I'll try again tomorrow."

"It's lovely," I say, because it is, or at least it would be if I wasn't too nervous to swallow. "Who did you make them for?"

Flavia looks puzzled. "Me, dear – well, and you as well, as it turns out!" She gives a deep, throaty chuckle.

"I thought people made toffee apples for little kids," I reply.

"Stuff and nonsense!" Flavia snorts, "I don't need an excuse to treat myself. Life is meant to be fun. It is, you know."

I know she is waiting.

"Look," I begin, not daring to meet her eyes, "I'm really, really sorry about the book – I'll buy you another one."

"You can't, dear, it's out of print," she says, standing up and reaching for the teapot.

"Oh no! I'm really sorry – I didn't . . ."

"Tell me," she interrupts, slopping milk into two mugs. "Do you feel better now?"

It isn't the question I had expected and I'm not ready for it.

"A bit," I say, without meaning to. "But it won't last."

Flavia fills the mugs with tea and pushes one in my direction. Aristippus, eyeing the milk jug with enormous interest, strolls over to his mistress and mews appealingly.

"Tell all," she says, filling a saucer with milk. It's not an order and I know if I refuse she will shrug her shoulders and tell me that's OK.

"I'm so angry!" I cry, dumping the half chewed toffee apple back on the plate.

"I spotted this," comments Flavia calmly. "About what, precisely?"

"I lost my cool with one of the teachers and now I've got to write an essay on self-control and . . ."

"Oh well, that's OK," she says calmly, sipping her tea. "We can do that together, no problem."

"What . . . you mean . . . we?"

She doesn't seem remotely shocked or surprised and waves a hand airily. "That's the easy bit," she says. "Go on. You were angry with the teacher. Why?"

Now I've started I can't stop. "The trouble is, nobody understands what's going on and they all think I'm just awkward. I told Amber – she's my best friend . . ."

"The one who wouldn't like my garden being tidy?" queries Flavia.

I grin despite my misery. "You remembered!" I say. "She used to think your undergrowth would be a good place for snogging!"

Flavia nods. "I suppose it would if you like that sort of thing," she says, totally unfazed. She's dead cool for an old person.

"Well, I told her that I was ill and having tests at the hospital and she found out that I was lying and got really upset with me."

"Well, she would," nods Flavia. "Why on earth did you tell her that?"

I wish I hadn't got myself into this but I can't think of a way out so I plough on. "Because she wanted to know why I was acting odd, and going off into daydreams and why my grades were so awful all of a sudden and – oh, everything!"

"I see. Help yourself to one of these, they are scrummy!"

She hands me a plate of warm chocolate brownies.

"Go on!" she says as I hesitate. "Spoil yourself!"

I take one and nibble on the edge.

"So why are you? Acting odd, as you put it," she asks.

"Because of Mum!"

There. It's out. And although I could retrieve myself I know deep down that there is no going back.

"She's not in China!" I say in a rush. "Or Hong Kong, or wherever it was I said she was."

I wait nervously for Flavia's reaction but she doesn't seem remotely shocked.

"So where is your mum?" she asks, biting into another biscuit. "Clearly somewhere you would rather she wasn't."

I swallow hard and my mind runs over the possibilities. Visiting my gran? On a cruise with her sister?

"In St Gregory's – the mental hospital."

I've said it. And I mustn't cry. I mustn't. So I bend down and stroke Ari and somehow it helps.

Flavia looks thoughtful. "Oh right," she says, as if I've just announced that Mum's popped to the hairdresser's for a quick cut and blow dry. "And that's why you lied to Amber – because you don't want anyone to know?"

"No, I don't!" I cry. "Only Amber made me promise always to tell her the truth in future, and I still can't tell her about Mum and if she found out . . ."

"Why not?" Flavia asks, looking genuinely puzzled. "Why can't you tell her?"

"Because everyone in my year thinks I'm weird anyway, and once they know Mum is in that place, they will realise that I've inherited it and I'm going insane too! And then I won't have any friends at all!"

Aristippus abandons the milk and stares at me with those huge, liquid eyes. Then he leaps on to my lap and begins kneading his paws into my thighs.

My own words ring in my ears and I realise for the first time that what I've just said is true. I know I'm mad, but no way can I let anyone else find out.

"So are they all crazy, these friends of yours?"

"What do you mean?" I ask. "Of course not. They're all normal."

"Oh," she shrugs. "I wondered – I mean, it seems to me that if they think you are insane, they must be somewhat off the mark themselves. You are as sane as I am."

I am not sure whether this is a compliment or an affirmation of my deepest fears.

"You don't know me," I mutter. "Sane people don't hurl things out of windows. Or trash their bedrooms. Or rip school books in front of the whole class."

I wait for the look of horror to cross Flavia's face, but her features don't move.

"Angry people do," she says. "Angry people scream and shout and stamp their foot and smash things. I once hurled a bottle of wine at a boyfriend. In the middle of his brother's wedding reception. Silly, really – it was such a waste of a decent claret. And it gave the bride's mother apoplexy!"

I can't help smiling.

"Losing your cool may not be the best way of dealing with the problem, but it sure doesn't mean you are crazy."

She reaches across the table and taps my arm.

"So," she says, "that's the size of it, is it? Mum's in hospital, and you are using up all your energy pretending she's not. You're worried sick about your mother because you love her, and yet you are lying to the one person who could see you through all this. Your best friend."

Put like that, what could I say?

"Yes, but . . ." I mutter, deciding that it is definitely time I was out of here. I dump Ari on to the floor and he stares at me in disgust.

"And what about your dad? We said hello, you know. On the pavement this morning. Nice man. Tired looking, though."

I smile non-committally.

"You've told him how you feel, have you?"

This is too much.

"I've tried, and much good it did me!" I jump up, pushing back my chair and stepping on Aristippus's outstretched paw. The cat wails in pain and leaps backwards.

"Oh, sorry, Ari!" I bend down, scoop him up and bury my head in his long white fur.

"All he says is that I have to be strong for his sake," I mutter, my voice muffled in Ari's fur. "Simon never rings me and Mum hates me . . ."

"We've done that bit," says Flavia calmly. "My guess is that your mum loves you to distraction and is worried sick about what you think of her. And that's a pretty scary thing for anyone, let alone a poor lass who is feeling down in the jolly old dumps."

I lift my eyes and meet her gaze. I've always thought that Mum was too wrapped up in her own misery to give a passing thought to me but if Flavia really is right . . .

"Well," she says briskly, "we've got to get this sorted, haven't we? First of all, you must talk to your mum and tell her how you feel."

"I can't . . ."

"Nonsense, of course you can! Maybe you won't, maybe you don't want to, but don't tell yourself you can't because that is just another lie!"

I open my mouth to reply and then shut it again. Frankly, I can't think of anything to say.

"Then you must tell Amber what's going on."

"But she might – well, it might put her off being my friend!" I retort. "I don't have many mates and I don't want to lose her."

"If she goes off you because your mother's ill for a wee while, she was never a friend in the first place," replies

Flavia. "Now – about this essay. Come over tomorrow after school and we'll make a start."

She rubs her hands in glee as if anticipating a night on the tiles.

Which reminds me.

"I can't," I say, "I've got a date."

It sounds cool, that does. I've never been able to say it out loud to anyone before.

"A date? How very sophisticated! Who's the guy?"

I shrug. "Don't know," I confess. "Amber set it up. Some mate of her boyfriend. She thought I needed cheering up."

"Well, there you are!" Flavia claps her hands. "Hardly the action of someone who thought you were insane, is it? So – pop in on Saturday and we'll do the essay then. And you can give me the low down on the mystery guy!"

I grin and nod. "Thanks for – well, the tea and – listening and stuff."

It doesn't come out the way it should but she seems satisfied.

"Take a couple of toffee apples with you, dear!" she says. "Sweet things are so consoling, don't you think? Share them with your mum on your next visit."

She stuffs two toffee apples into my pocket and ushers me to the door. "Take this with you," she says, proffering the mudstained picture book. "I'd like you to have it."

She opens the door and grabs Aristippus as he tries to make a dash for the garden.

"Oh look!" she cries. "There's your father!"

Dad is striding up the steps to our house two at a time, laden with briefcase and carrier bags.

Flavia waves expansively. "Hi there, Lawrence!"

Good grief, she's on first name terms with him already.

"Been to see your wife? How is she today?" She beams at him expectantly.

I can see that my father hasn't a clue how to respond. He looks from Flavia to me and back again and rubs his nose.

"It's OK, Dad, I've told her about Mum," I say.

And do you know, his whole face seems to relax in an instant. His shoulders drop, and he stands a bit taller. It's really strange. You would have thought that he'd be embarrassed but he doesn't seem bothered at all.

"Oh. I see. That's great. Yes, she's much better today, thank you," he says, turning to Flavia. "The doctors feel they've turned a corner with her."

"Splendid, splendid!" cries Flavia. "Onward and upward, then!"

And with that she gives another wave and shuts the front door, missing Ari's tail by a millimetre.

"Nice woman," murmurs Dad, putting his key into the lock.

"Yes," I reply. "She is. Really nice."

The funny thing is, she's made me think that, perhaps, if I really give it a go, I could end up being quite nice too.

Weird.

"I got us a takeaway," Dad says, gesturing towards the

bags he has dumped on the kitchen table. "So you wouldn't have to cook."

So he listened to me after all.

"Ace!" I exclaim. "Chinese?"

He nods and grabs cutlery from the kitchen drawer. Things are looking up – my father is laying the table.

"Your favourites – crispy duck and seaweed, pork with bamboo shoots and loads of prawn crackers. Will that do?"

I grin and nod. "Sorry about earlier," I mumble. "I'll try harder, I promise."

"Good girl," he says.

We eat in silence for a few minutes and I try to think just how I'm going to say the next bit.

"Dad," I begin, "about that woman I saw you with."

"Jenny?" he queries. "What about her?"

"Are you having an affair with her?"

He drops his cutlery and looks at me in amazement.

"What a ridiculous question!" he retorts. "Of course I'm not! How could you think such a thing of me?"

He is staring at me as if I have just descended from another planet.

"Is that really what you think of me? Have I been such a useless husband and father that you believe I would do something so – so –"

He is at a loss for words.

"I'm sorry," I am forced to say. "It was just that, seeing you kiss her . . ."

"It was just a friendly gesture," he protests. "She'd cheered me up, let me talk about Mum, get everything off my chest. That's all."

It sounds a hell of a lot to me, but I don't say anything. At least he's not going to run off with her, which is all that matters, I guess.

"I can't believe you said that, Georgie," he continues. "I'm devastated."

He puts down his fork and runs his fingers through his hair. "How could you – and today of all days?"

I can feel the anger building but I am determined to keep calm.

"What's so special about today?" I ask.

Dad gets up and wanders over to the fridge. "They've offered me a transfer," he says. "To the Newcastle office."

"Newcastle?" That's miles away. He can't do that.

"Jenny thinks I should take it," he adds, grabbing a can of lager from the fridge. "Jenny sees it as a positive way forward."

"Well bully for flaming Jenny!" I shout. "You can't do that, Dad! We live here, this is our home. And besides, what about Mum?"

He pulls back the ring-pull and takes a long slug of the lager. "She'd be proud of me, wouldn't she?" he asks with a note of pleading in his voice. "I mean, Newcastle is a bigger office, a larger area to cover. And I'd get more money."

I swallow hard. I don't want to move. OK, so Kettleborough might not be the gateway to the world, but it's the only place I've ever lived and Amber's here and I might be going to fall in love tomorrow.

"I don't know what to do, Georgie," he says. "What do you think?"

I'm about to tell him but he's rambling on.

"I mean, you want me to do what's best for Mum, don't you? And a new house, fresh start – that might be just what she needs."

He pauses and rubs his nose. "And of course," he adds brightly, "Mum would love to be so close to Simon – Durham's only a few miles from Newcastle, you know."

I say nothing. Suddenly the crispy duck tastes like soggy cardboard.

"Georgie? I need you to help me out on this one."

He's looking at me with that droopy spaniel expression, as if I'm the one with all the answers. I wish.

"Dad, I can't. It's not my problem. You'll have to talk it over with Mum, OK?"

"But if she's going through a bad patch . . . ? I mean, I don't want to upset her . . ." he stammers.

"But it's fine to upset me, is that it? Dad, I don't know what's right. I don't want to move away but that's not the point. The point is that it's your job, your decision and your problem. Not mine. Get it?"

Dad shrugs his shoulders. "If that's the way you feel," he mutters.

"It is, Dad," I tell him. "It is. And now I've got homework to do. I'll see you later. Thanks for supper."

And with that I get up and walk out of the room.

I'm dead chuffed with myself. I did it. I said it how it

really was. And the funny thing is, there wasn't a coloured cloud in sight.

It's only when I slump down on the bed that another cheering thought strikes me. This Jenny woman can't be passionately in love with Dad, because if she was, she wouldn't be encouraging him to go hundreds of miles away.

Cool.

But he still shouldn't have kissed her like that.

FRIDAY

Of course, the state of euphoria I was in last night hasn't lasted. It might have done, if it hadn't been for the fact that within half an hour of waking up this morning, I had discovered a zit the size of the Millennium Dome on my chin, listened to my brother spouting a load of rubbish down the phone and had a close encounter with that demented cat next door.

Simon had rung when Dad was in the shower.

"Look," he said, launching into this great spiel as soon as I picked up the phone, "I'm really sorry about the other night. I didn't mean to sound hard."

"Oh really!"

No way was I going to make it easy for him, not after the way he had been.

"It's just that I haven't told Serena about Mum and . . ."

"You were in bed with her!" I retorted, gripping the receiver until my knuckles turned white.

"Georgie!" Simon sounded fazed.

"Oh come on, Simon," I replied. "I'm not a kid any more – I'll be sixteen next week, if you remember, which I doubt. You had been making love to this Serena girl and couldn't hack being rumbled by your kid sister, right?"

"Your timing could have been better," he admitted.

"And the fact that I'm stuck here, coping with a loony mother and a father who is rapidly losing the plot, doesn't come into it, right? Well, don't worry, Sy, because I can cope. I don't need you! I don't need anyone!"

"Georgie, listen. I know I've been a bit . . ."

"Simon, I don't have time for all this. I have to get Dad's breakfast, iron a shirt for him and get to school, all by eight forty-five, OK? I'll talk to you next week."

Of course, once I'd hung up, I wished I hadn't. He is my brother and I love him, and half of me wishes I'd said that I was falling apart and couldn't handle any of it. But something stopped me. I don't know what. Maybe knowing that once he does get home, Mum won't have any time for me at all. And before that happens, I have to go and talk to her.

Just like Flavia said.

I wouldn't have seen Flavia this morning if it hadn't been for Aristippus. Never mind hedonist, that cat certainly doesn't have a homing instinct. I crashed downstairs in a tearing hurry, with Dad asking for toast and eggs double quick, and there he was – lying on the bottom stair, fast asleep. Aristippus, not Dad.

Well, he was asleep until I fell over him. Then he leaped a metre into the air, claws outstretched, hissing madly.

Well, to cut a long story short, I fed him milk and last night's leftover Chinese and got Dad sorted, and then I took him back next door. Aristippus, not Dad.

Flavia opened the door and she looked dreadful. I mean, really awful. Her eyes were red and her hair was standing up on end.

"Oh, thank God!" She grabbed Ari and buried her face in his fur.

"He was asleep on our stairs when I came down this morning," I began. "I'm so sorry – I guess he must have slipped in when Dad got the takeaway and we never spotted him."

She looked up and there were tears in her eyes.

"It's all right, dear," she said. "My fault, not yours. I really thought I'd lost him this time. I must be more vigilant."

She clutched him tightly to her huge bosom and smiled at me. "You must think I'm daft," she said, her voice stronger again. "It's just that Ari is very precious to me."

"Have you had him long?" I said, more for something to say than because I was interested.

"Six years," she said and there was a catch in her voice. "Ari was the last present my son gave me before he died."

★ ★ ★

I'm almost at the school gates now, and I can't get it out of my mind. I mean, I'd never thought of Flavia having children. She said she'd given up on men and I just assumed she was an old spinster. But apparently she had this son by a guy she met in Greece when she was almost too old to have children. The guy didn't want to know and Flavia brought up the kid on her own.

"He was twenty-one when he died," she told me. "He was at university, doing so well. And then one night, he and some mates went to a party, the car hit some black ice and he was killed outright."

I can't stop thinking about it. Twenty-one and dead. That's the same age as Simon. It could have been Simon. He's forever going all over the North East to raves and parties and things.

"We'd had a row a couple of weeks before," Flavia told me. "Aristippus was a sort of making up present from David. He brought this little kitten for me on the Sunday before he went back to uni."

She closed her eyes for a moment and sighed. "By the Friday, he was dead."

I don't want to think about it, but in my head I keep hearing the words Flavia said as she waved me off to school. "I'm so glad we made up," she said. "I'm so glad we said how much we loved one another."

Of course, Sy's not going to die, and neither is Mum. It's silly to think like that.

But I'll phone Simon back tonight.

And after school, before I go out with Amber, I'll nip in to see Mum.

That's what I'll do.

I don't see Amber to talk to until after lunch. When we do catch up with one another, she starts gabbling away before I have time even to start the speech I've been practising all morning in my head.

"Look, I'll be round tonight at seven, OK? Now wear something really sexy and alluring."

I search my memory but can't come up with a single item that fits the bill.

"Like what?" I ask.

"Oh – I don't know!" she says. "How about your black satin skirt with the pink cropped top – the one that plunges."

I pull a face. "Sadly, there's not a lot for it to plunge to," I mutter.

Amber giggles. "Just wear it," she says. "Must dash, I've got . . ."

I grab her arm. "Listen – there's something I want to talk to you about," I begin.

Amber grins. "If you want a run-down on this mate of Nick's you are out of luck," she chuckles. "All I know is that he's at college and is rebuilding some old car with Nick and his brother."

"No, it wasn't that . . . it's about . . . well, you know . . . yesterday, after I'd told you about . . ."

"Forget it – we've sorted that! Look, I must dash," she

gabbles. "Nick's stuck on his German translation and he's always *so* grateful when I help him. He just can't cope without me! See you tonight!"

She's gone and I haven't told her about Mum. Still, that's not my fault, is it? I'll tell her tonight when she comes to fetch me. Then we won't have any secrets and everything will be OK.

I guess I've blown it again. It was OK to start with – we talked about Mum's class and how she feels better now they've changed her pills. She even said she was sorry about getting in a state and I said forget it, because what else could I say?

I should have left it at that and gone home. Only being me, I didn't.

She hasn't said a word since I asked the question. She's just sitting there, staring at me.

All I asked was, "Do you love me, Mum?"

It's not Mastermind.

"Mum?" I need her to answer. I need to know.

"Oh, Georgie!" she bursts out. "Of course I do. You'll never know how much."

"So tell me!"

I didn't mean it to come out like that – only how can I know if she won't say how it is?

"I know you don't love me as much as Simon," I begin, "but do . . . ?"

"Don't!"

That's it. One word. Don't. And what's that supposed to mean? Don't talk about it? Don't admit that you know I don't love you as much as your brother?

She's starting to cry now and I can't hack this. I edge towards the door.

"Darling, wait!" Suddenly she sounds quite balanced, assertive even. "Sit down – please."

I sit.

She stretches out and takes my hand. "I love you, Georgie, so much that sometimes it hurts," she says, wiping away her tears with her free hand. "I never meant to be such a rotten mother, you know – I never meant to let you down like this."

"You're not . . ."

"No wait," she interrupts, squeezing my hand. "I need to explain something. Since I've been in here, I've been able to talk to my psychiatrist and I'm facing up to things like never before."

"What things?"

"Georgie, when Simon was born I rejected him."

"Rejected him?" This I can't believe. Mum has doted on Simon for as long as I can remember.

She closes her eyes and for a moment I think she's going to clam up on me, but then she gives herself a little shake and looks up. "I had post-natal depression," she says. "Very badly. I wouldn't feed him or cuddle him – I just didn't want to know. I'll be honest – it was Dad who was keen to start a family, not me. I resented the baby."

"But you got over it?" I ask. "I mean, after a few weeks."

She shakes her head. "No," she says. "It was months – well, over a year, actually. I had a nanny for him and I went back to work and gradually, with the help of pills, the depression lifted. But I never really bonded with Simon after that."

I can't get my head round this. "But, Mum, you've always loved Simon more than me and . . ."

"No!"

For one awful moment I think she's going to flip but she seems OK.

"Georgie, listen to me. When Simon was five, I fell pregnant with you. I didn't mean to . . ."

"Oh, thanks!"

". . . but when you were born, it was like someone had flicked a switch inside my head. Everything fell into place. I adored you on sight. I couldn't get enough of you."

For some reason my eyes are watering.

"Really?" It comes out as a whisper.

"Really," she says. "I took maternity leave and I wouldn't let you out of my sight. Simon was at school by then and the nanny had gone, and it was just you and me at home. It was wonderful – you were so cute!"

She smiles in a way I haven't seen her smile for ages.

"And then the trouble started," she sighs, the smile fading.

"You went off me?"

"No! Never!" She takes a deep breath. "I suddenly

realised that all those years, I hadn't given poor little Simon one tenth of the attention or care that I was lavishing on you. I felt so guilty. I was determined to make it up to him, to somehow blot out the memory of that depressed, uncaring mother and be the perfect parent to him from that minute on."

I know that before she says another word I have to ask the question again. I must hear her say it properly. I have to.

"So you still love me? Really?"

"Georgie, I love you more than words can say. I just wish I hadn't behaved in such a way that you felt the need to ask."

She gets up and walks to the window and I know it's because she doesn't want me to see the tears in her eyes, so I pick up a magazine from the table and flick through it.

"I always felt bad about neglecting Sy when he was little," she said. "I guess I went over the top trying to make it up to him – always praising every little thing he did, bragging about his achievements to anyone who would listen, buying him stuff . . ."

I let out a long, slow breath. It's beginning to make sense. And she does love me.

"It all started going wrong when you went to school," she says suddenly. "I went back to full-time work – I'd been doing two days a week until then – and within a month, Dad lost his job. He got another one – but his confidence never picked up. He had four jobs in five years and none of them paid very well."

I remember Dad's words – *"She had to put her all into her career and now she's burned out."*

"So it was all down to you?" I ask softly.

She nods. "I was working all hours God made, and missing you and – yes, by then – Simon too, and the depression started again. Only worse. I had it in my head that if I had another baby I could get it right this time, somehow wipe out all the mistakes I'd made with you and Sy. I know it sounds stupid . . ."

I jump up and hug her before I know what I'm doing. "No, Mum, it doesn't sound stupid," I cry. "Just unnecessary. We love you. You're a great mum! But I don't understand . . ."

"What?"

"Well, I don't want to upset you or anything but . . ."

"You won't, I promise," she says with a smile.

"In Norfolk that year, when you hit Dad and threw things – and then all those other times when you screamed and ran out of the house and kicked and . . ." I falter. I don't reckon I should be saying this to my own mother.

Mum sits down and puts her head in her hands.

"I used to feel so guilty, so useless – a waste of space," she explains. "Twice in my life I'd got pregnant when I didn't want to – and then, when I had set my heart on it, it simply didn't happen."

I can see it now. Mum yelling at him, calling him useless, saying she hated him.

"The doctors have made me see the truth now," Mum

continues, "that the anger I hurled at you and Dad was really anger I wanted to hurl at me. I would tell Dad he was useless because he couldn't hold down a high-powered job – but really I envied him because he spent time with you and Simon and he had his painting and photography and – well, he was well-rounded as a person."

Now this I do need to get my head round. Of course, Dad did do things with us, tobogganing and kite flying and go-karting and stuff. And he always had time to help with homework, unlike Mum, who would sit up half the night writing reports or sending faxes. But he never did anything without asking Mum how to do it first.

"Dad couldn't have been a good dad if you hadn't been there, keeping us all together," I say. And as the words come out, I know that for once in my almost sixteen years, I've got it right.

Mum smiles and slowly walks over to me. She wraps me in her arms and hugs me as if she will never stop.

I don't want her to stop.

Nothing ever felt so right.

I'm halfway home before I realise that I haven't mentioned my birthday. But I don't care. Mum loves me. Before I left she told me that the doctors are really pleased with her, and that it won't be long before she comes home.

I'm not going to think about that bit too much right now. I mean, I'm pleased, of course I am, but I'm a bit scared too. What if the rows start up again? What if she hears about my bad behaviour at school and flips and it sends her back into that depression? What if she and Dad argue about him going to Newcastle? I didn't tell her about that. It's not my problem.

So I won't think about her coming home, not yet. I'll just keeping focusing on the fact that she loves me.

And I love her.

Very much.

CHAPTER SEVEN

FRIDAY
evening

I'm in a state. A whole battalion of butterflies are hurtling around my stomach and it's not just because in forty-five minutes I'll be meeting this guy and trying to think of something scintillating to talk about.

I'm in a stew because Amber has just phoned to say she's running late, and can we meet outside the cinema instead? Which is fine except that I had made up my mind to come clean with her, and tell her the whole truth about Mum. Well, maybe not all of it – not the bits about her throwing things and stuff – but certainly the truth about her being in St Gregory's and suffering from depression.

And now I can't. I mean, there is absolutely no way I'm going to say all that stuff in front of Nick and this mate of his.

So I guess it will have to wait until tomorrow.

I suppose it doesn't matter. After all, I've lied for so long, one more day can't do any harm, can it?

Amber waves frenetically as I jump off the bus. I dash across the road and she grabs my arm.

"You cut it a bit fine, didn't you?" she accuses me. "They'll be here any minute. Do I look all right? Is this skirt too short? Should I have worn thicker tights?"

"Yes, no, and no," I laugh. "You look terrific. What about me?"

I do a twirl.

"Ace. Amazing," she replies, eyeing me in surprise. "You seem in a good mood – what's changed?"

I wonder for a moment whether there is time to tell her – but just as I'm about to launch into the story, she looks over my right shoulder, clamps her hand to her mouth and grabs my arm.

"There they are! Over there! Now, Georgie, give this your best shot, OK?"

She grabs the other arm.

"Wow! That guy is something else. He's a dish! Look!"

I turn and peer up the road. Nick is waving at Amber and beside him is a tall guy – no. Oh, please God, no. It can't be.

"Hi, darling!" Amber's voice becomes higher and much more breathy, the way it always does when she's speaking to anyone of the opposite sex.

Nick kisses her.

I want the ground to open right now and swallow me up for all eternity. I can't do this.

Nick turns to me. "Hi, Georgie!" he says. "This is . . ."

"I know," I say and it comes out as a squeak. "Hi, Leo."

Amber looks gobsmacked.

"Hey!" Leo cries, his face creasing in a broad grin that makes him look sexier than ever. "It's you – the runaway girl from the hospital!"

"Hi!" I say weakly.

"You *know* one another?" Amber demands accusingly, as if I had spoiled her fun on purpose.

I can't bear it. I have to tell Amber. Everything. Right now. I can't bear for her to discover the truth like this – by accident – again. It's so unfair! She's bound to think that I've been lying despite all I said and she'll never trust me again. I turn to Amber.

"Amb, there's something I need to tell you," I begin, my voice wobbling. "I've been trying to tell you for days now – but there was never the chance. It's that . . . well . . . it's my mum. She's the one in hospital. In St Gregory's. That's how I know Leo. He's doing work experience there."

"Your mum? In St Gregory's? But she can't be! You said she was in Hong Kong."

Amber says each word slowly, emphasising every syllable. She is not smiling.

"I know. I know. I'm sorry. I just couldn't face anyone knowing – not even you."

"But you promised! No more secrets, remember! And

you sat in my house and told my mum she was abroad!" she shouted. "My mum couldn't work out why yours hadn't rung or written – she always used to! And then . . ."

"Just listen, will you?" I can't help shouting back. "I'm really sorry. I've tried so many times to tell you, but it's not easy, you know. It's not the kind of thing you can just drop into the conversation."

Nick sniffs. "I guess not," he says and for a moment I think he's going to make Amber see sense. "I wouldn't want to brag if my mum was a psycho."

He titters and blows bubblegum out of the side of his mouth.

That does it.

"Oh, get lost!" I shout. "Both of you. I don't need this, OK? I . . ."

"Nick, that was out of order!" Leo has taken a step towards him.

Amber looks like she is going to cry, like she doesn't know what to do. For a moment Nick says nothing. Then he drops his eyes and stares at the pavement.

"Sorry," he says, kicking an empty Coke can with his toe and looking at me out of the corner of his eye.

"Look," says Leo calmly, "let's just go and see the film and relax a bit. We'll have to get a move on if we're not going to miss it."

I smile at him gratefully and turn to Amber.

"Amber . . ."

I touch her arm nervously.

"Oh God, I'm so sorry, Georgie," she cries. "You poor thing."

Enveloped in her hug, I know that everything will be OK. I haven't blown it. Amber will forgive me – and Leo hasn't run off yet . . .

In fact, as we walk into the cinema, Leo moves closer and puts his arm round my shoulder.

"Are you OK?" he asks gently. "I guess it must have been tough for you – and idiots like Nick mouthing off doesn't help . . ."

"I guess that's why I wouldn't tell anyone," I admit. "Funny though – now it's happened, it doesn't seem as bad as I thought it would be. I can handle it."

Leo grins at me. "I can see you've got your mum's guts!" he says. "She's an amazing woman, you know – and she has me in stitches sometimes, she's so funny."

I smile. "She used to tell the most cringe-making jokes," I admit.

"What do you mean, used to?" laughs Leo. "She still does. She's getting better all the time, Georgie. I know I'm not meant to talk about the patients – but I heard Dr Morgan say that Julia Linnington was a success story in the making."

"Really?"

"Really," he smiles. "Now – one more question?"

"What?" I ask anxiously.

"Popcorn or jelly beans?" he asks.

★　★　★

The film was dire. I mean, awful. Which was cool because halfway through Leo suggested that he and I went for a coffee instead and the look on Amber's face as we shuffled our way past her and Nick and headed up the aisle to the exit had to be seen to be believed.

Now, standing in front of my dressing-table mirror, trying to work out whether I look different now that I'm in love, I can hardly believe what happened. We went to Costa Coffee and Leo bought me a cappuccino and a cinnamon whirl. We just talked and talked, about everything under the sun, except Mum. And that was cool too because I found myself chatting about me. Me, the person – not me, the daughter with difficult parents, or me the Year Eleven failure. It was the oddest thing – I found myself remembering all the things I want to do; silly things like going to Alton Towers or learning salsa dancing and big things like training to be a beauty therapist and working on a cruise liner and seeing the world. It was as if I'd been living in a sort of limbo land for months and suddenly, I could think straight.

"So, can I see you again?" Leo asked when we had finished our coffee. "Tomorrow afternoon? We could go for a walk and talk some more."

I know you're not meant to sound too eager, but when you've had as few invitations as I have, you don't take any chances.

"Yes," I said. "Oh. No."

Leo's face fell. "Why? What's the problem?"

I didn't tell him about the trashing session; I just said that I had an essay to write and how Flavia said she'd help.

"No probs," he declared. "You go to this Flavia lady and come out with me afterwards. I'll pick you up. What time?"

So tomorrow, at six o'clock, Leo's coming to fetch me. That's in twenty hours and seven minutes' time.

He is so cool and so fit. And he's been just so incredible about everything – like me and Amber yelling at each other within five minutes of meeting him! I really didn't believe boys could be so amazing. And the strangest thing of all is that I feel so comfortable with him. I've never been like that with guys before – but with Leo I feel as if I don't have to pretend.

And for me, that's quite something.

I'm wrecked. It's been a wicked day. Mum and me are sorted and I've fallen in love. The only worry is Amber. I mean, she seemed OK at the cinema but I haven't had the chance to check it out. I'll call her tomorrow.

And then there's my birthday to sort out.

Now there's a thought.

I wonder . . .

SATURDAY

It's taken me all day to work out what's different. Apart from being madly and desperately in love, that is.

And I've just sussed it.

I haven't talked to myself. Not once. And I haven't floated off on any clouds, although that nearly happened this morning.

Dad and I went to see Mum together. It was funny really – Dad said he was popping along to the hospital and I said that I'd go too. His face was a picture but he seemed really chuffed.

"She's ever so much better," I said as he parked the car outside the main entrance. "You'll be gobsmacked."

Only it didn't turn out that way. When we got to the day room she was sitting gazing out of the window, and although she smiled and tried to make conversation, she was uptight, biting her fingers and fidgeting with her watch strap all the time. Not that Dad was a great help; he went on and on about some boring sales meeting and kept patting her hand and saying, "So how are you?" over and over again.

"There's something I want to ask you about, darling," he said suddenly and I knew he was going to talk about Newcastle. I had told him not to; I'd begged him to leave it for a few days, until Mum was completely all right again, but he said that decisions had to be made and that his boss was pressing for an answer.

"How would it be if we all . . . ?" he began, and that's when a small murky grey cloud appeared just above my right eye.

"I'll go and get some coffees," I said hastily, because you can't afford to waste time with clouds. "Want one, Mum?"

"If you like," she said vacantly, picking at the cuff of her blouse.

I was heading back with the coffees, trying to pretend the cloud wasn't following me, when Miranda Jenks appeared from one of the consulting rooms.

"Georgie!" she cried, as if I was her long lost cousin. "Lovely to see you! How's things?"

A week ago I would have had the sense to say, "Fine," and carry on with getting the coffee. But she was standing right beside me and suddenly I reckoned that I deserved a few answers.

"I don't get it," I said. "Yesterday Mum was great –

almost like her old self, but today she's all distant and edgy again. Why?"

Miranda smiled. "These things do take time, Georgie," she said. "Look – sit down for a second and let me try to explain."

She ushered me into her office and gestured to me to sit in one of the saggy armchairs. "Your mum has been facing up to a lot of things that happened in her past," she began.

"I know," I interrupted, because no way was I going to let her think that Mum didn't love me enough to tell me what had been going on. "About rejecting Simon and then making it up to him and all that."

"She told you? That's brilliant!" Miranda looked really pleased. "The fact that she can talk about it to the one person she wants to love and admire her is such a step forward."

"What? Say that again."

"Which bit – that your mum is desperately frightened that she has blown it, and that you will think of her as a failure and drift off to university and never get in touch?"

"She said she loved me," I said, without meaning to.

"Did you ever doubt it?" asked Miranda.

I nodded.

"She adores you," Miranda stated simply.

"But why is she worse again today?" I demanded.

"Don't you ever have a bad day?" asked Miranda. "The sanest, most well-balanced people on earth have good days, bad days and absolutely dire days – why shouldn't

Mum? She's faced a lot of things that are painful and she's done it with great courage. Give her a break!"

I smiled and nodded. But there was one more question I had to ask. "So – it's not hereditary, then?"

I remember that I stared at my lap while I said it, and held my breath waiting for the answer.

She took her time about it and I began to dread the worst.

"Georgie, there is no way that anything your mum has been through can be passed on to you. That's not to say that you will never feel depressed, never have times in your life when you will feel furious with the entire universe . . ."

"I do already," I confessed.

"Oh goody!" laughed Miranda. "That proves one thing, then."

"What?" I asked, wondering what she was on about.

"That you're as normal as the next person," she said. "Now get those coffees to your parents before they die of thirst!"

So I did.

On the way home in the car I asked Dad what Mum had said about Newcastle but all he would say was that he had sown seeds, whatever that might mean. Anyway, when I said goodbye to Mum she hugged me as if she really meant it and even sent her love to Amber and told me to let Joy know that she would be in touch soon. Amazing.

When we got home, there was a message on the answerphone from Leo. Of course, it was Dad who played it and so I got the Spanish Inquisition about who this guy was, and did he come from a decent home, and was it really a good idea for me to be consorting (his word, not mine) with a boy I knew nothing about? So I told him that Leo was doing work experience at St Gregory's and knew Mum and had been really kind when Nick spouted a load of rubbish, and that appeased him somewhat.

It was when he embarked on his idea of a fatherly chat about attractive young girls and virile young men that I decided enough was enough.

"Got to dash, Dad," I said. "Flavia's going to help me with my homework."

And with that I fled.

The funny thing is, I'm really looking forward to it. Well, not doing the essay exactly, but telling Flavia everything. I can't wait.

"Blueberry muffins or fruit loaf?" Flavia demands before I've even taken off my jacket. "New recipes, don't know how they've turned out but we simply can't work on an empty stomach. So which is it to be?"

"Whichever you're having," I begin politely, and then remember. "No. I'll have some fruit loaf, please. Toasted. With jam."

She roars with laughter and thumps me on the back. "You're learning!" she cries. "Jolly good show – fruit loaf it is!"

She ushers me into the kitchen. Aristippus is curled up

on a chair and blinks at me in a rather snooty manner.

"So how was the blind date?" Flavia enquires, slicing fruit loaf and putting it in the toaster. "Was the guy fit?"

She's really clued up for someone of her age. Dad thinks fit means being good at athletics.

"To die for," I sigh. "And he's asked me out later. So I have to be home by six – he's picking me up."

"Oh terrific!" she cries. "I can peer out of the window and give him the once-over! And how is your mother – did you have a chat?"

I nod. "She does love me," I say. "And she explained so much – but I don't know whether I should tell you. I mean . . ."

Flavia waves a hand at me. "My dear, I wouldn't dream of letting you. It's your mother's private concern and nothing to do with me. Just as long as you two are in tune again?"

"We are," I say. "I don't even mind that she's forgotten about my birthday . . ."

"Birthday? Not today, surely?" Flavia gasps, jumping up to rescue the toast.

"Next weekend," I tell her. "She had said, ages ago before she flip– before she became ill – that I could have a big party. Sweet sixteen and all that – like they do in America."

"And?" Flavia looks at me in a puzzled manner and dumps pots of jam on the table.

"Well, of course, now I can't because she's in hospital and Dad's too agitated about work and stuff."

"I see," Flavia says. "Well, well."

She looks thoughtful for a moment and then shakes herself. "Come on, then – to work! Bring your plate through to my den and we'll get going! Self-control, eh? Terrific!"

She is lovely – but sometimes I'm perfectly sure the woman is totally mad.

I can't believe it. If you had asked me two hours ago how writing an essay scored as a fun thing to do, on a scale of one to ten, I would have given it minus five. But this is ace.

When we sat down Flavia got out a pile of coloured paper and thrust it at me.

"Forget the dreary exercise book," she demanded. "We'll use this."

"We're not allowed . . ." I began.

"Did this man – what's his name?"

"Mr Lamport," I tell her.

"Did Mr Lamport say you had to write in this book?"

I shook my head.

"So we won't," she declared. "Coloured card is far better for what I have in mind. Now – a quotation, I think."

"Pardon?"

"I always believe in starting an essay with a quotation," she explained. "For one thing, your teacher will be highly impressed and for another, you will have learned something. Get my *Dictionary of Quotations* – it's over there, next to *The History of Britain*."

And that's how it started. We looked up self-control and found that loads of famous people had opinions about it.

That's how my essay came to start with the words: *When angry, count four; when very angry, swear.*

Mark Twain said that. He wrote *Tom Sawyer* and *Huckleberry Finn*. Flavia was horrified when I said I'd never read them so she's lent them to me. They're really battered books, with weird pen and ink drawings. I think they're a bit old-fashioned but she says they are really good stories, so I'll give them a go.

Anyway, we've nearly finished. I've written it all down – about how being scared can make you angry and how sometimes you act before you think. I've said that self-control can be a bad thing – especially when it stops you expressing your innermost feelings or prevents you from admitting that you're hurting inside.

It's a dead clever essay, even if I say so myself.

I leap up and hug Flavia without thinking. "Thanks a million," I smile.

"You are most welcome, dear," she says. "But remember our little pact?"

I swallow hard. "Do you think it's really necessary?" I ask.

"I know it is," she says. "It could make all the difference."

I sigh. It won't be easy. In fact, it will be the hardest thing I've done.

"OK," I whisper. "I'll give it a go."

I can always change my mind on Monday morning.

And I don't have time to worry about it right now.

Right now, all I'm concerned about is getting glammed up for Leo.

I can't take my eyes off him. I know it's corny, but when he looks at me, my knees turn to water and I tingle in places I didn't know you could tingle.

It's been the most amazing evening. I mean, we didn't do anything special. We walked along the canal for what seemed like miles and then stopped at this wacky pub on the waterfront and had Titania's Dreams, which are wicked non-alcy cocktails, served with paper umbrellas and sparklers.

"How old are you?" Leo asks me suddenly as we settle down to a second round. "I mean – do you want something stronger?"

I shake my head. "I'll be sixteen next Saturday," I tell him and his eyebrows shoot upwards.

"Sixteen?" he gasps. "I thought you were older than that."

Here it comes. Now he's going to make polite going home noises and that will be that. I'll never see him again.

"Is that a problem?" I say tightly, not daring to meet his eyes.

"Of course not," he replies. "Why should it be?"

Then he takes my hand. I think I might have stopped breathing.

"You're lovely," he remarks, quite simply. "Whatever age you are."

He sips his drink. "So how will you be celebrating?" he asks. "Wild party? Family gathering?"

I shrug. "Nothing, I guess," I say. "To be honest, I'm in a right mess over my birthday."

I can't believe I said that. This is the guy I want to impress more than anyone else on this planet and I'm about to come clean about the fact that I'm a liar and a fraud.

I'm keeping quiet.

"Go on," he urges.

"I told my mates that my mum was throwing this big party for me and now she's in hospital, and I can't have it and I look a total nerd."

So much for keeping quiet.

"Say you've changed your mind and are doing something much more original instead," he suggests. "That'll shut them up."

"Well . . ." I begin and then stop. I can't say it. I mean, I've been thinking about it for twenty-four hours but putting it into words is something else.

"What?"

"I was wondering, I don't suppose – but no, of course you can't! It's stupid!"

Leo frowns. "Can't what?"

I take a deep breath. "Well, could you possibly, next Saturday, just for one day – well, an evening really – or even just a couple of hours would do it . . ."

"Georgie! What are you trying to say?"

This is it. Please, God, don't let him hate me.

"Could you pretend to be my boyfriend?"

There. I've said it.

"No," Leo says.

Well, thank you very much, God. My stomach lurches and I can feel my face turning scarlet.

"No, well, I shouldn't have asked . . ."

"No, I can't pretend to be your boyfriend," he says, grinning at me. "But I could do something else."

"What?"

Nothing else will do.

"I could be your boyfriend," he says. "Georgie, I think you're great. I want to spend time with you. Lots of time. Could you bear for us to be an item?"

I stare at him. He wants me as a girlfriend. This dishy, fit, gorgeous, lovable, friendly guy wants me – Georgia Linnington, loony of Year Eleven – to go out with him.

Thank you, God. I didn't mean to get at You. I'll never, ever stop believing in You ever again, I promise.

"Yes, please," I breathe and he takes my hand and leans towards me.

If he's about to do what I think he is about to do, I might very well die and go to heaven.

I close my eyes and he does it.

I've been kissed.

And if I'm not very much mistaken, he's about to do it all over again.

AND NOW . . .

Sunday

Well, I've heard of women in the olden days pining away for their lovers and dying of consumption on a *chaise longue* in some Victorian drawing-room but this is ridiculous. I've been dreaming of Leo all night long and now I can't move. My legs feel like lead and there's a brass band playing in my head and my throat is on fire.

I am going to die. But at least I've been kissed.

Monday

God is very unfair. He has had fifteen years and eleven months in which to give me what Dr Myers calls a viral throat infection and I call death – and He chooses the one week when I've fallen in love and need to be at my prettiest, wittiest and sexiest.

Some chance.

The worst part is that I promised to phone Leo and I can't speak. Not even a squeak.

He'll think I've gone off him and he'll find someone else.

I'm going to die.

Not of my sore throat, just of a broken heart.

Tuesday

I am so happy, I could die. Leo called round! To see me! With a huge bunch of flowers and a little chocolate teddy bear with "Get Well Soon" painted on his tummy.

Dad was dead iffy about letting Leo into my bedroom and kept hovering on the landing, but I sent him down to get drinks and that was when Leo kissed me.

I croaked something about him catching my germs but he said anything that came from me would be worth having.

Wasn't that romantic?

I'm so happy.

In between feeling like death, that is.

Wednesday

I can talk again – after a fashion. Leo says my voice is very sexy now that it's gone husky. I might try and keep it that way.

The best bit is that he says I have to be completely well by Saturday – my birthday. He's taking me out! He won't say where, but I don't care, because when I go back to school tomorrow, I'll be able to tell Caitlin and Rebecca and the others that I'm going out with my boyfriend.

And this time, it won't be a lie.

Thursday

I feel sick. It's not because of the throat infection – that's gone and I'm back at school. It's because Mr Lamport has demanded to read the essay.

There was no, "How are you, Georgina dear?" or "So sorry you were ill." He has just marched into the classroom to take us for PSE, fixed me with one of his steely gazes and demanded to know whether I've written the required number of words.

I swallow hard.

"Well?"

"Yes, sir," I say.

"Then hand it over," he orders.

I am so tempted to do just that, but I remember what Flavia said and I take a deep breath. "Please, sir, I would like to read it out to the class," I say, my voice shaking. "I think I owe it to everyone – my friends – to let them know what happened."

I can see that he is about to refuse but I keep going. "The truth, this time," I say. "All of it."

There isn't a sound. Everyone is looking at me.

"Very well," agrees Mr Lamport and his voice isn't quite so stern now. "Go ahead."

I walk to the front of the room with my pile of coloured cards. I fix my eyes on Amber because I know she will be on my side and I start.

"*When angry, count four; when very angry, swear.* Mark Twain wrote that years and years ago – he was a clever guy most of the time, but that piece of advice was dumb. I know. I did it. And it got me into big trouble . . ."

They are listening. I guess that's because they are too gobsmacked to do anything else. After all, it's not often that I do anything in front of the class apart from act weird.

I carry on reading. My voice is getting firmer and I move on to the second and then the third coloured card.

Now it's the difficult bit.

"My mother is in a psychiatric hospital." I pause. I can hear the odd gasp. Even Mr Lamport looks a bit taken aback.

"I was stupid enough to believe that it was something to be ashamed about, something to keep secret," I read. "But it's not. It's no more shameful than having a broken leg or German measles or . . ."

And here I look straight at Liam. ". . . a faceful of acne." The class laughs.

"When we talked about mental health in class," I go on, "I got really uptight. That's when I lost it – self-control."

I take a deep breath. "I have told a load of lies lately – I'm not having tests in hospital, my mum isn't abroad and there won't be a birthday party on Saturday."

At this point Rebecca and Caitlin and Emily burst out laughing, and I see Amber kick one of them under the table. I guess they think it's a right riot that I'm caught out, but I carry on reading.

"Self-control is about facing up to facts in a dignified way, and from now on that is what I shall be doing," I read. "I lashed out in class and I'm sorry. Really."

I've finished.

I sit down.

Suddenly everyone is clapping — even Mr Lamport, which has to rate as the eighth wonder of the modern world.

"Georgie, well done!" he booms. "That took courage, Class, great courage and I'm sure we are all very proud of Georgie!"

Rebecca and Caitlin are smiling at me, nudging one another. I'm not sure whether that's good or bad, but right now I don't care.

I did it.

I told the truth.

And everyone's still speaking to me.

Ace.

CHAPTER TEN

SATURDAY

I'm sixteen. I've been sixteen for exactly one hour and twenty-five minutes – only so far no one except Dad seems to have noticed.

He and Mum got me this wicked CD Walkman and a huge card saying "To our Beautiful Daughter" which was cool.

But no one else has done anything.

I thought Sy would send a card but the postman has been and gone. I have a nasty feeling he's still angry with me. I should have phoned him. I'll do it later.

I do love him. He is my brother, after all.

Apart from the usual ten-pound book token from my grandmother in Cornwall and a card from Auntie Rachel in Doncaster, that's it.

Nothing from Amber – but then again, she might pop

round later. And of course, Leo will be coming this evening to take me out.

And that will make up for everything.

I love him so much.

I wish it was seven o'clock now.

Leo's phoned! He sang Happy Birthday down the phone – it was so cute. And he wants to pick me up at five o'clock because he says he can't wait till seven.

Isn't that romantic?

He still won't tell me where we're going, but he said dress up and look glammy.

I've got to phone Amber. I don't do glammy very well.

Amber was dead weird. I mean, she wished me a happy birthday and everything but she didn't say anything about a pressie – and when I asked if I could go round and have a rummage through her clothes, she said she had loads to do and it wouldn't be very convenient.

I even offered to help her but she changed the subject and said she had to dash.

Never mind.

I've got Leo and that's all that matters.

He'll be here any minute. I hope I look OK. I had planned to spend all afternoon getting ready – defuzzing my legs, giving myself a French manicure, the lot – but Dad suddenly decided to take me out to lunch and we've only been back half an hour. We weren't eating all that time, of course – but when we'd finished, Dad said why didn't we go and see Mum, and I could hardly say no, could I?

We needn't have bothered – when we got there, she was nowhere to be seen and Miranda pulled Dad to one side and muttered something in his ear, and he looked all pink and flustered.

"She's in a class," he said hastily.

"On a Saturday?" I was instantly suspicious. "She's worse, isn't she?"

"No!" Miranda interrupted. "Honestly, Georgie, she's fine. And Dad got it wrong – she's having a . . ."

She paused for an instant. "A massage," she said. "To relax her. Why don't you come back later?"

And with that she winked at Dad in what, frankly, was a fairly forward manner.

"I'm going out later," I said loftily. "With my boyfriend."

She looked at Dad and for one moment I thought she was going to start asking all sorts of questions.

"Out?" she asked.

"Yes," said Dad hastily. "Just for a bit."

Honestly, there are times when I think the whole lot of them need psychological treatment.

Anyway, we finally got home, and I've done my hair. It looks cool, even though I say so myself. I copied this picture of Cate Blanchett at some film première and I reckon I look pretty sophisticated, in an understated and rather classy sort of way.

I'm wearing my black skin-tight dress (the one Dad doesn't approve of) and strappy sandals and I've done my nails six different colours and stuck transfers on. They are still wet, thanks to Dad's timing, but with a bit of luck . . .

The bell! He's here! Oh my God!

"Leo!" I can hear Dad's voice. "Now listen, old chap, I thought we should have a little chat . . ."

I'm off. Now. You never can trust parents to talk sensibly when you want them to.

Leo is so smooth. He even ordered a taxi to take us to – well, wherever it is we are going. It must be costing him a fortune – we've been driving for ages. Not that I mind, because he's been holding my hand, stroking my hair and telling me how great I look.

"Here we are!"

It's a pub with a thatched roof and wooden tables outside. Oh, I'm not disappointed or anything – it's just that I thought we might be going to some cool club.

"Wait a minute, won't you?" I hear Leo mutter to the driver, although I can't think why. He sees me eyeing him.

"Just want to make sure everything is OK for you," he gabbles.

We walk hand in hand through the door of the pub and then Leo slams his hand to his chest.

"Oh no!" he gasps. "My wallet – I must have left it at your place!"

He looks devastated.

"But you were hardly in the house five minutes," I say. "Are you sure it's not in the taxi?"

He scoots back to have a look and then shakes his head dismally. "There's nothing for it," he says. "We'll have to go back."

"No, we won't," I reply. "I've got five pounds and . . ."

"That's not enough!" He almost barks the words and drags me back to the taxi, shoving me inside.

"Back to Phillimore Gardens, please."

The driver seems dead chuffed and gives him a big wink. I guess he reckons he's on to easy money tonight.

"I'm so sorry, darling," Leo sighs, slipping his arm round my shoulder and kissing my nose. "Forgive me?"

"Of course," I assure him. "We can still do something special later, though, can't we?"

"You bet," he says and gives me another, longer kiss.

And after that, I frankly don't care what we do.

"I'll wait here," I tell Leo when the taxi pulls up outside my house.

"No!" Leo sounds so worried and immediately I feel guilty. The poor guy is probably worried sick about the fare. "Anyway, I'll need you to help me find the wallet."

It's not until I'm halfway up the steps to the front door that I realise the taxi has driven off.

"Leo!" I gasp. "You never paid him."

"I'll sort it later," he mutters. "Have you got a key?"

I unlock the door and step into the hall.

"Where do you think you left it?" I ask him.

"In the sitting-room," he answers at once. "Go and look, will you?"

He pushes me ahead of him, and I open the door.

And stop dead.

The room is full of people and balloons, and party poppers are going off all over the place.

"Happy birthday, Georgie! Surprise, surprise!"

I can't believe it. They are all there – Amber and Nick, Rebecca, Emily and Caitlin – the whole class practically.

"Didn't you guess? Did it work, Leo? We thought we'd never be ready in time!"

Everyone is gabbling at once and I'm laughing and crying at the same time, and Leo is dragging me further into the room, gesturing to the far end by the conservatory door.

I stare. And blink. Twice.

Standing by the door, dressed in the burgundy velvet trouser suit that I love the most, is Mum.

She is clutching a glass of something fizzy and smiling from ear to ear.

And she looks dead normal.

"So it was all a set-up – the taxi and you pretending to forget your wallet and everything!" I gasp laughingly to Leo. "How did you do it?"

He grins. "It was mainly down to Flavia," he says. "When I left your place the other day, she called me over and said she wanted to do something for your birthday but didn't think it was her place to interfere. So I had a word with your mum at the hospital – and she told your father."

"So that's why he took so long over lunch!" I gasp. "So you could get ready!"

Leo grins. "He knew your mum would be having her hair done when you called in - but it was a way of wasting some more time!"

"And you did all that for me?" I whisper.

He squeezes my hand. "Why not?" he asks. "That's what you do for people you care about, isn't it?"

I am about to whisper something romantic when my dad claps his hands. "Quiet, everyone!" he shouts, and I start praying that he isn't going to do anything embarrassing. "Make way for the cake!"

The door opens and there's Flavia, looking – well, amazing really – in a sort of lime green caftan with dozens of purple beads round her neck and a sort of feather helmet thing on her head.

"Georgie – happy birthday!"

She beams at me and dumps an enormous cake on the table. Everyone gasps. It's in the shape of a cat, iced in white with a huge red bow round its neck. And it is lying on an open book.

"It's Aristippus!" I cry.

"Ari-who?" asks Amber, who is already salivating at the sight of the cake.

"My cat, dear," murmurs Flavia. "Without Ari, I might

never have got to know Georgie properly."

"And without the book . . ." I begin, winking at Flavia.

"Precisely!" she laughs, grinning back at me. "Anyway, enough chatter! Let's light the candles!"

She has just lit the sixteenth candle when the doorbell rings and Mum leaps out of her seat.

Leo catches her eye and she sits down again.

"Georgie – go and see who that is and tell them we're busy," says Dad.

I hurtle into the hall, desperate to get rid of whoever it is, and fling open the door.

"Hi, sis," says my brother. "Sorry I'm late – the trains were . . ."

But what happened to the trains I never discover. I am too busy being squashed in a Polo-scented hug.

It's been the best evening ever. Caitlin is being really nice to me but I rather think that has something to do with the fact that she hasn't taken her eyes off Simon ever since he arrived. Rebecca actually chatted to Mum and then told me how sorry she was for being so mean to me.

"I guess I was just jealous," she said. "I've never had a party and I suppose getting at you was my way of handling it. Sorry."

I told her it was OK and I meant it. We all do stupid things sometimes.

There's only one thing – Mum's beginning to look pretty edgy. I can see her picking at the cuff of her top, the way she always does when things start to get too much for her. And she keeps swallowing and glancing at her watch.

I push my way across the room, past Emily and Marcus, who are snogging for England, and squat down by Mum.

"Why don't you go back now, Mum?" I suggest as gently as I can. "You look tired and besides, this lot will be carrying on for ages yet."

She looks at me and then up at Dad, who has appeared with a glass of water.

"Well . . ." You can see she wants to escape but I know she's afraid I'll be upset.

"I could go upstairs to lie down," she offers. "Or . . ."

"You'll feel better going back to the hospital, Mum," I say quietly. "It won't be for much longer, will it? In a couple of weeks you'll be home – hopefully to a quieter house than this!"

She smiles and touches my hair. "Thanks, darling," she says. "You do believe I love you, don't you?"

"I know you do, Mum," I say. "Just like I love you."

Dad helps her up and turns to me. "We'll slip away when no one's looking," he says. "No big deal."

I nod.

Leo slips his hand in mine. "Come and dance," he says. "I've driven a lot of miles to make this evening happen."

"The taxi!" I cry as he drags me to the other end of the room. "You never paid . . ."

"Yes, I did!" he laughs. "Or rather, Flavia did. She set it up – paid the guy in advance. It was all her idea."

I turn round to thank her but Leo clutches me tightly and pulls me towards him. His lips caress my neck.

I'll thank Flavia later.

Right now I have other things to think about.

By the time we stop dancing, Mum and Dad have gone. I leave Leo talking boring car talk to my brother and slip into the kitchen.

Flavia is sitting at the kitchen table, staring at a photograph.

She looks up as I walk in. "David," she says simply and thrusts the picture into my hands.

A blond, smiling boy with a mass of freckles and a turned up nose smiles back at me. Flavia's son.

"He's very handsome," I say. "Was – I mean."

"Leave it as 'is'," whispers Flavia. "I like to imagine he's around, watching me, saying, 'Oh mother, really!' the way he used to."

I can see that her eyes are bright with unshed tears. I walk up to her and give her a hug.

"Are you all right?" I ask.

She shakes herself and beams. "I'm fine, dear," she assures me.

"Mum's gone," I tell her. "Back to the hospital."

I chew my lip. There's so much I want to say. I want to thank her for being there, for never being too pushy. I want to tell her that I understand Mum and Dad more now and that I don't have to take sides or choose between them. I can love them both – and I can see both of them for what they really are. I guess that's what being grown up is about.

Flavia clearly thinks that I'm upset because Mum's gone.

"She's so much better, Georgie, that's what your father told me," she says. "She will be home very soon."

"I know," I nod, smiling at her.

"And what about you, Georgie?" she asks me. "Are you OK?"

I take a deep breath and think about it.

"Yes," I tell her and I'm surprised at how relieved I feel. "Yes, I am OK. Really I am."